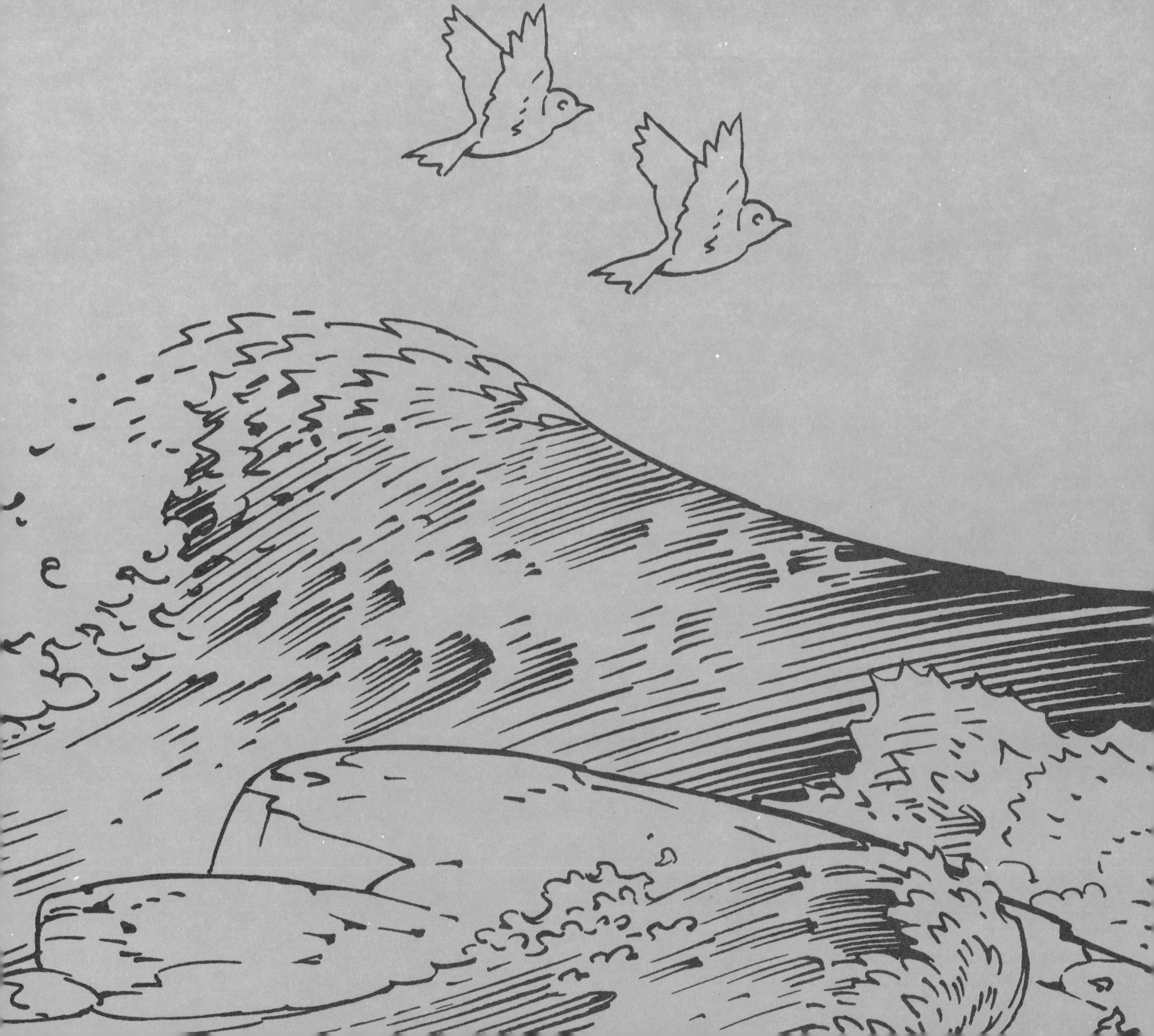

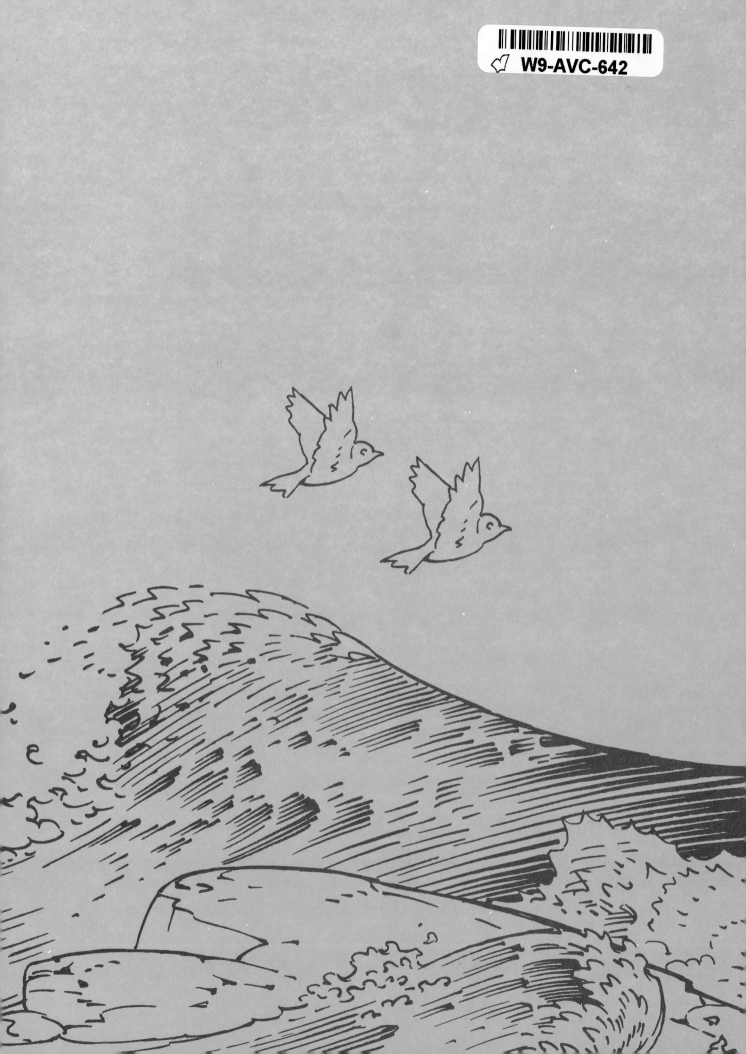

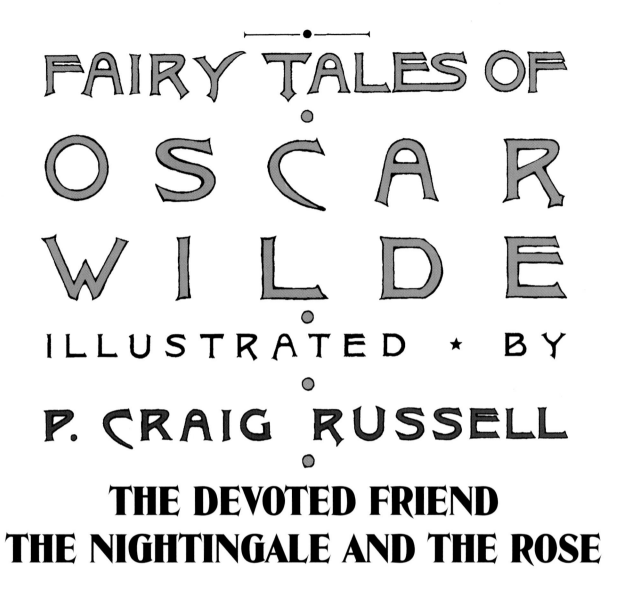

FAIRY TALES OF OSCAR WILDE

ILLUSTRATED ★ BY

P. CRAIG RUSSELL

THE DEVOTED FRIEND
THE NIGHTINGALE AND THE ROSE

NANTIER · BEALL · MINOUSTCHINE
Publishing inc.
new york

Also available by P. Craig Russell:
FAIRY TALES OF OSCAR WILDE
Vol.1: The Selfish Giant and The Star Child, $15.95 hc., $8.95 pb.
Vol.2: The Young King and The Remarkable Rocket, $15.95
Vol.3: The Birthday of the Infanta, $15.95
THE JUNGLE BOOK, $16.95
OPERA ADAPTATIONS:
Vol.1: The Magic Flute, $24.95 hc., $17.95 pb.
Vol.2: $24.95 hc., $17.95 pb.
Vol.3: $24.95 hc.
($3 P&H 1st item, $1 each addt'l)

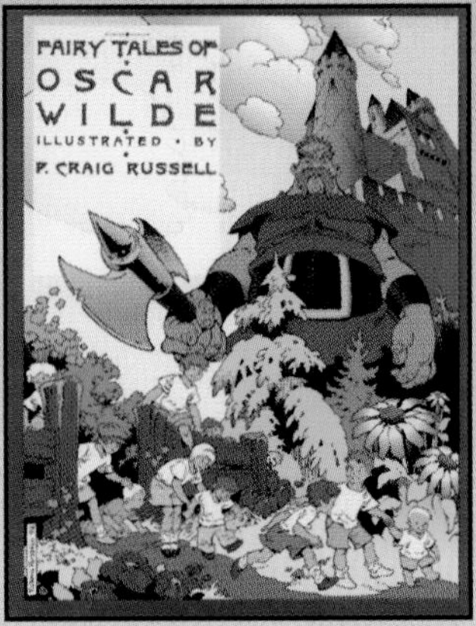
FAIRY TALES OF
OSCAR
WILDE
ILLUSTRATED · BY
P. CRAIG RUSSELL

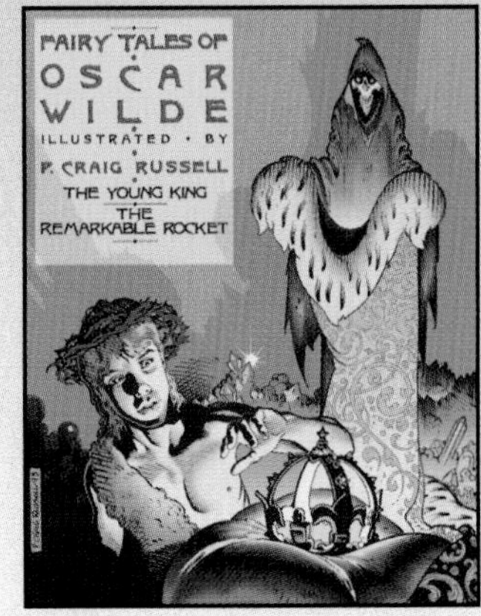
FAIRY TALES OF
OSCAR
WILDE
ILLUSTRATED · BY
P. CRAIG RUSSELL
THE YOUNG KING
THE
REMARKABLE ROCKET

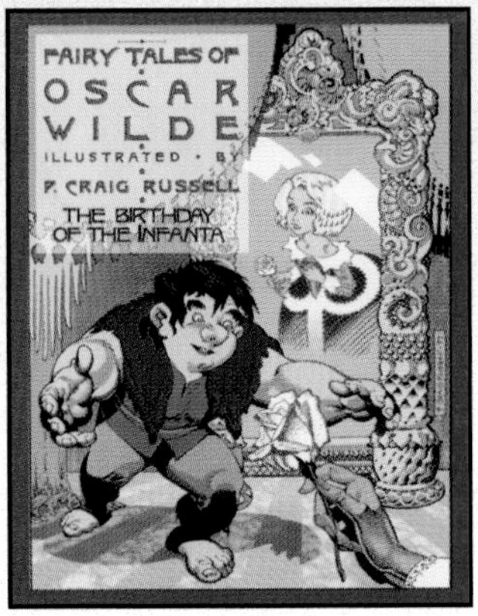
FAIRY TALES OF
OSCAR
WILDE
ILLUSTRATED · BY
P. CRAIG RUSSELL
THE BIRTHDAY
OF THE INFANTA

Send for our free color catalog:
NBM, dept. FT
555 8th Ave., Ste. 1202
New York, NY 10018
www.nbmpublishing.com/tales

ISBN 1-56163-391-7, cloth
ISBN 1-56163-392-5, paperback
ISBN 1-56163-376-6, signed & numbered
Library of Congress Control Number: 93229468

Lettering by Ortho
Colors by Lovern Kindzierski
Printed in China

3 2 1

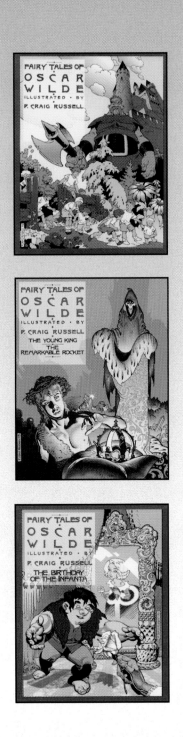

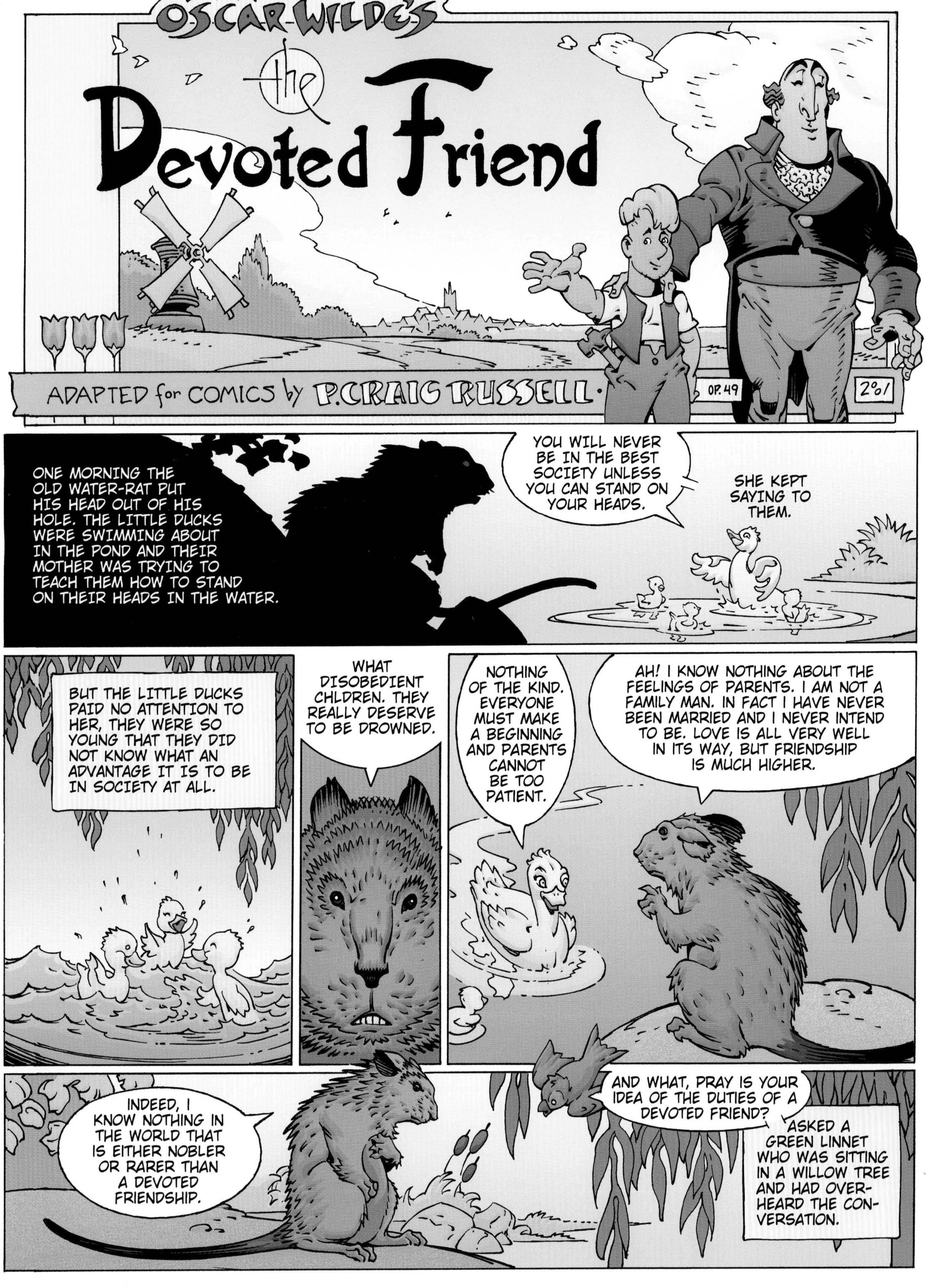
OSCAR WILDE'S
the Devoted Friend
ADAPTED for COMICS by P. CRAIG RUSSELL
OP. 49
2 of 1
ONE MORNING THE OLD WATER-RAT PUT HIS HEAD OUT OF HIS HOLE. THE LITTLE DUCKS WERE SWIMMING ABOUT IN THE POND AND THEIR MOTHER WAS TRYING TO TEACH THEM HOW TO STAND ON THEIR HEADS IN THE WATER.
YOU WILL NEVER BE IN THE BEST SOCIETY UNLESS YOU CAN STAND ON YOUR HEADS.
SHE KEPT SAYING TO THEM.
BUT THE LITTLE DUCKS PAID NO ATTENTION TO HER, THEY WERE SO YOUNG THAT THEY DID NOT KNOW WHAT AN ADVANTAGE IT IS TO BE IN SOCIETY AT ALL.
WHAT DISOBEDIENT CHLDREN. THEY REALLY DESERVE TO BE DROWNED.
NOTHING OF THE KIND. EVERYONE MUST MAKE A BEGINNING AND PARENTS CANNOT BE TOO PATIENT.
AH! I KNOW NOTHING ABOUT THE FEELINGS OF PARENTS. I AM NOT A FAMILY MAN. IN FACT I HAVE NEVER BEEN MARRIED AND I NEVER INTEND TO BE. LOVE IS ALL VERY WELL IN ITS WAY, BUT FRIENDSHIP IS MUCH HIGHER.
INDEED, I KNOW NOTHING IN THE WORLD THAT IS EITHER NOBLER OR RARER THAN A DEVOTED FRIENDSHIP.
AND WHAT, PRAY IS YOUR IDEA OF THE DUTIES OF A DEVOTED FRIEND?
ASKED A GREEN LINNET WHO WAS SITTING IN A WILLOW TREE AND HAD OVER-HEARD THE CON-VERSATION.

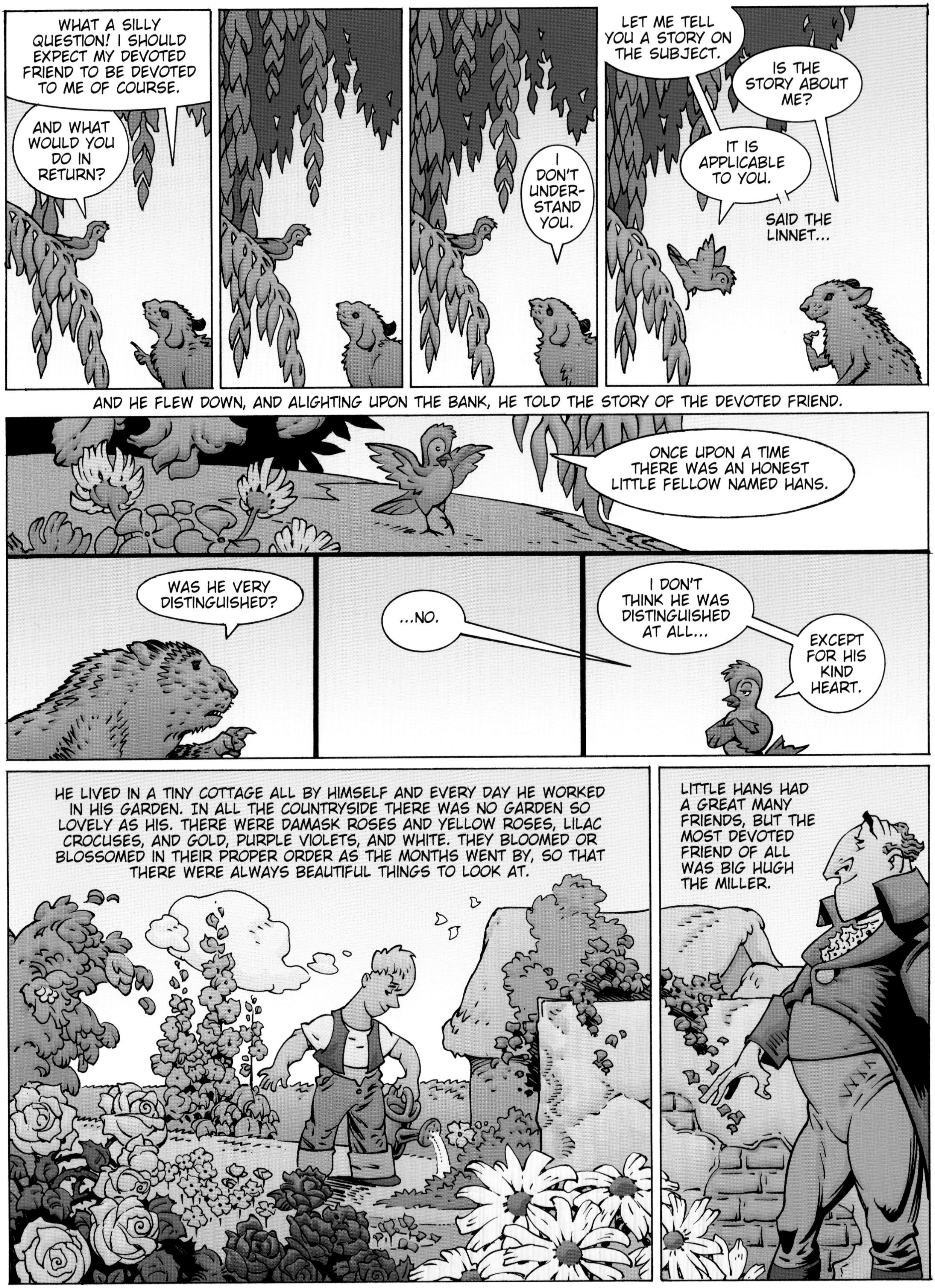
WHAT A SILLY QUESTION! I SHOULD EXPECT MY DEVOTED FRIEND TO BE DEVOTED TO ME OF COURSE.
AND WHAT WOULD YOU DO IN RETURN?
I DON'T UNDER-STAND YOU.
LET ME TELL YOU A STORY ON THE SUBJECT.
IS THE STORY ABOUT ME?
IT IS APPLICABLE TO YOU.
SAID THE LINNET...
AND HE FLEW DOWN, AND ALIGHTING UPON THE BANK, HE TOLD THE STORY OF THE DEVOTED FRIEND.
ONCE UPON A TIME THERE WAS AN HONEST LITTLE FELLOW NAMED HANS.
WAS HE VERY DISTINGUISHED?
...NO.
I DON'T THINK HE WAS DISTINGUISHED AT ALL...
EXCEPT FOR HIS KIND HEART.
HE LIVED IN A TINY COTTAGE ALL BY HIMSELF AND EVERY DAY HE WORKED IN HIS GARDEN. IN ALL THE COUNTRYSIDE THERE WAS NO GARDEN SO LOVELY AS HIS. THERE WERE DAMASK ROSES AND YELLOW ROSES, LILAC CROCUSES, AND GOLD, PURPLE VIOLETS, AND WHITE. THEY BLOOMED OR BLOSSOMED IN THEIR PROPER ORDER AS THE MONTHS WENT BY, SO THAT THERE WERE ALWAYS BEAUTIFUL THINGS TO LOOK AT.
LITTLE HANS HAD A GREAT MANY FRIENDS, BUT THE MOST DEVOTED FRIEND OF ALL WAS BIG HUGH THE MILLER.

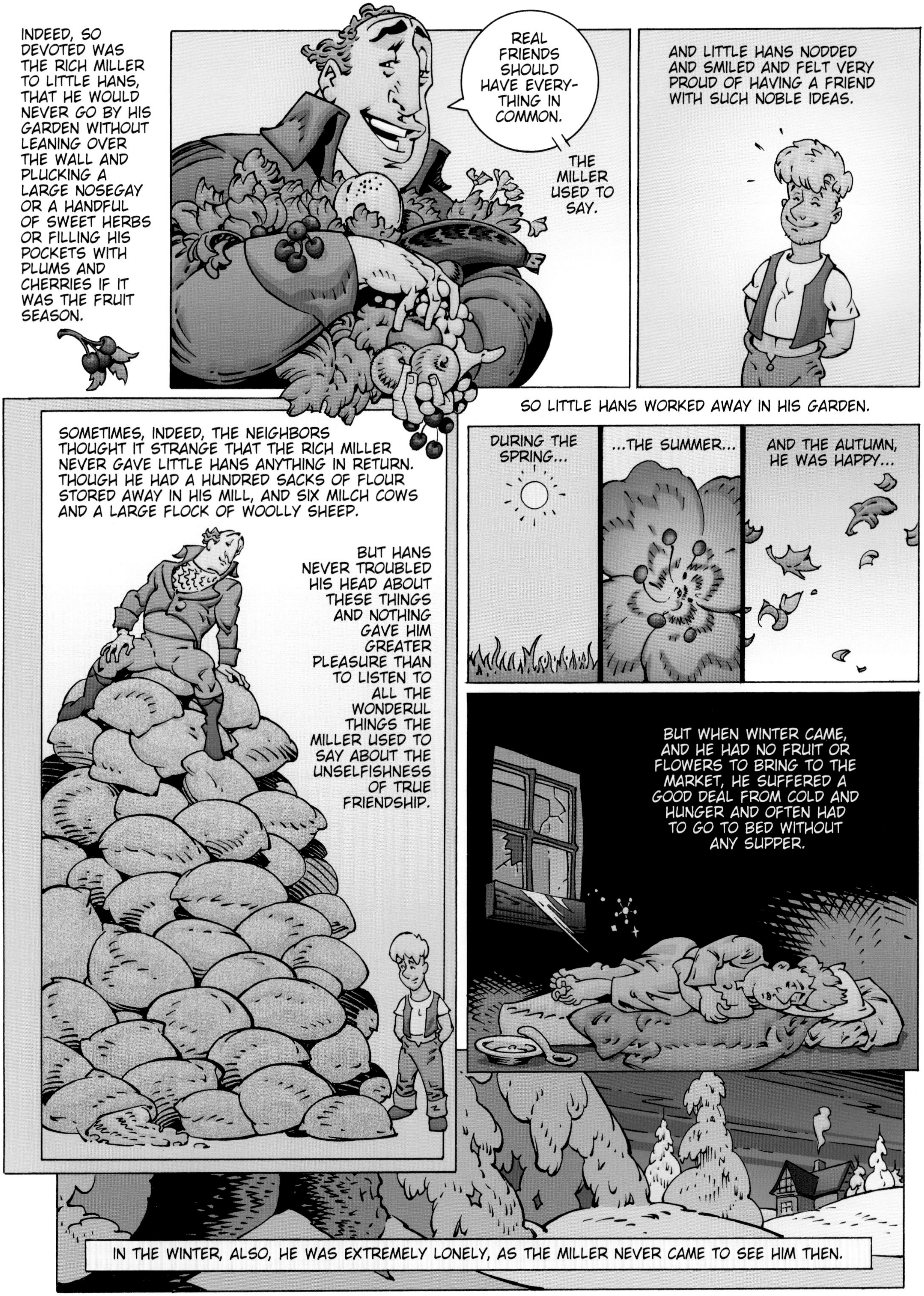
INDEED, SO DEVOTED WAS THE RICH MILLER TO LITTLE HANS, THAT HE WOULD NEVER GO BY HIS GARDEN WITHOUT LEANING OVER THE WALL AND PLUCKING A LARGE NOSEGAY OR A HANDFUL OF SWEET HERBS OR FILLING HIS POCKETS WITH PLUMS AND CHERRIES IF IT WAS THE FRUIT SEASON.
REAL FRIENDS SHOULD HAVE EVERY-THING IN COMMON.
THE MILLER USED TO SAY.
AND LITTLE HANS NODDED AND SMILED AND FELT VERY PROUD OF HAVING A FRIEND WITH SUCH NOBLE IDEAS.
SOMETIMES, INDEED, THE NEIGHBORS THOUGHT IT STRANGE THAT THE RICH MILLER NEVER GAVE LITTLE HANS ANYTHING IN RETURN. THOUGH HE HAD A HUNDRED SACKS OF FLOUR STORED AWAY IN HIS MILL, AND SIX MILCH COWS AND A LARGE FLOCK OF WOOLLY SHEEP.
BUT HANS NEVER TROUBLED HIS HEAD ABOUT THESE THINGS AND NOTHING GAVE HIM GREATER PLEASURE THAN TO LISTEN TO ALL THE WONDERUL THINGS THE MILLER USED TO SAY ABOUT THE UNSELFISHNESS OF TRUE FRIENDSHIP.
SO LITTLE HANS WORKED AWAY IN HIS GARDEN.
DURING THE SPRING...
...THE SUMMER...
AND THE AUTUMN, HE WAS HAPPY...
BUT WHEN WINTER CAME, AND HE HAD NO FRUIT OR FLOWERS TO BRING TO THE MARKET, HE SUFFERED A GOOD DEAL FROM COLD AND HUNGER AND OFTEN HAD TO GO TO BED WITHOUT ANY SUPPER.
IN THE WINTER, ALSO, HE WAS EXTREMELY LONELY, AS THE MILLER NEVER CAME TO SEE HIM THEN.

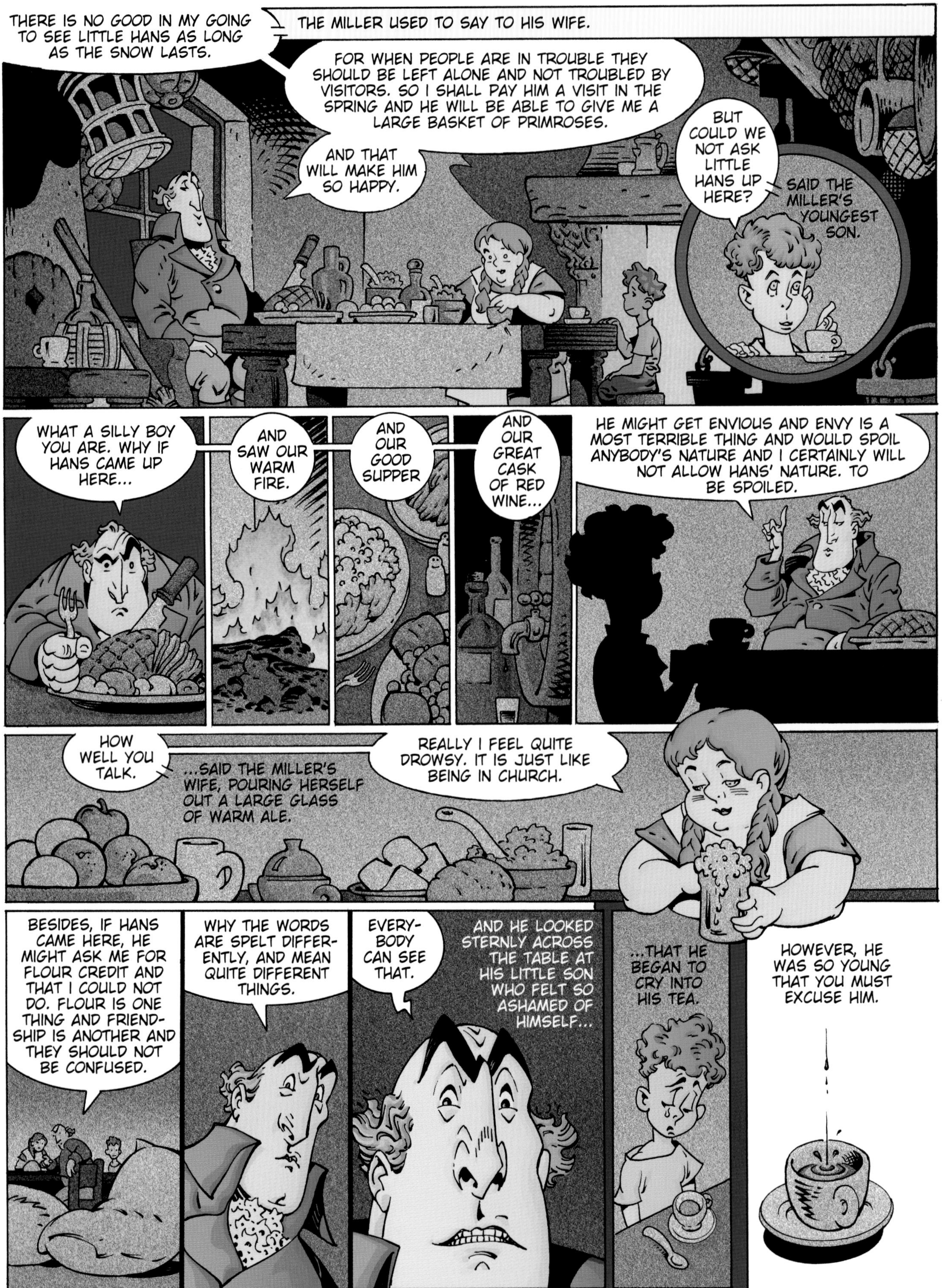
THERE IS NO GOOD IN MY GOING TO SEE LITTLE HANS AS LONG AS THE SNOW LASTS.
THE MILLER USED TO SAY TO HIS WIFE.
FOR WHEN PEOPLE ARE IN TROUBLE THEY SHOULD BE LEFT ALONE AND NOT TROUBLED BY VISITORS. SO I SHALL PAY HIM A VISIT IN THE SPRING AND HE WILL BE ABLE TO GIVE ME A LARGE BASKET OF PRIMROSES.
AND THAT WILL MAKE HIM SO HAPPY.
BUT COULD WE NOT ASK LITTLE HANS UP HERE?
SAID THE MILLER'S YOUNGEST SON.
WHAT A SILLY BOY YOU ARE. WHY IF HANS CAME UP HERE...
AND SAW OUR WARM FIRE.
AND OUR GOOD SUPPER
AND OUR GREAT CASK OF RED WINE...
HE MIGHT GET ENVIOUS AND ENVY IS A MOST TERRIBLE THING AND WOULD SPOIL ANYBODY'S NATURE AND I CERTAINLY WILL NOT ALLOW HANS' NATURE. TO BE SPOILED.
HOW WELL YOU TALK.
...SAID THE MILLER'S WIFE, POURING HERSELF OUT A LARGE GLASS OF WARM ALE.
REALLY I FEEL QUITE DROWSY. IT IS JUST LIKE BEING IN CHURCH.
BESIDES, IF HANS CAME HERE, HE MIGHT ASK ME FOR FLOUR CREDIT AND THAT I COULD NOT DO. FLOUR IS ONE THING AND FRIENDSHIP IS ANOTHER AND THEY SHOULD NOT BE CONFUSED.
WHY THE WORDS ARE SPELT DIFFERENTLY, AND MEAN QUITE DIFFERENT THINGS.
EVERYBODY CAN SEE THAT.
AND HE LOOKED STERNLY ACROSS THE TABLE AT HIS LITTLE SON WHO FELT SO ASHAMED OF HIMSELF...
...THAT HE BEGAN TO CRY INTO HIS TEA.
HOWEVER, HE WAS SO YOUNG THAT YOU MUST EXCUSE HIM.

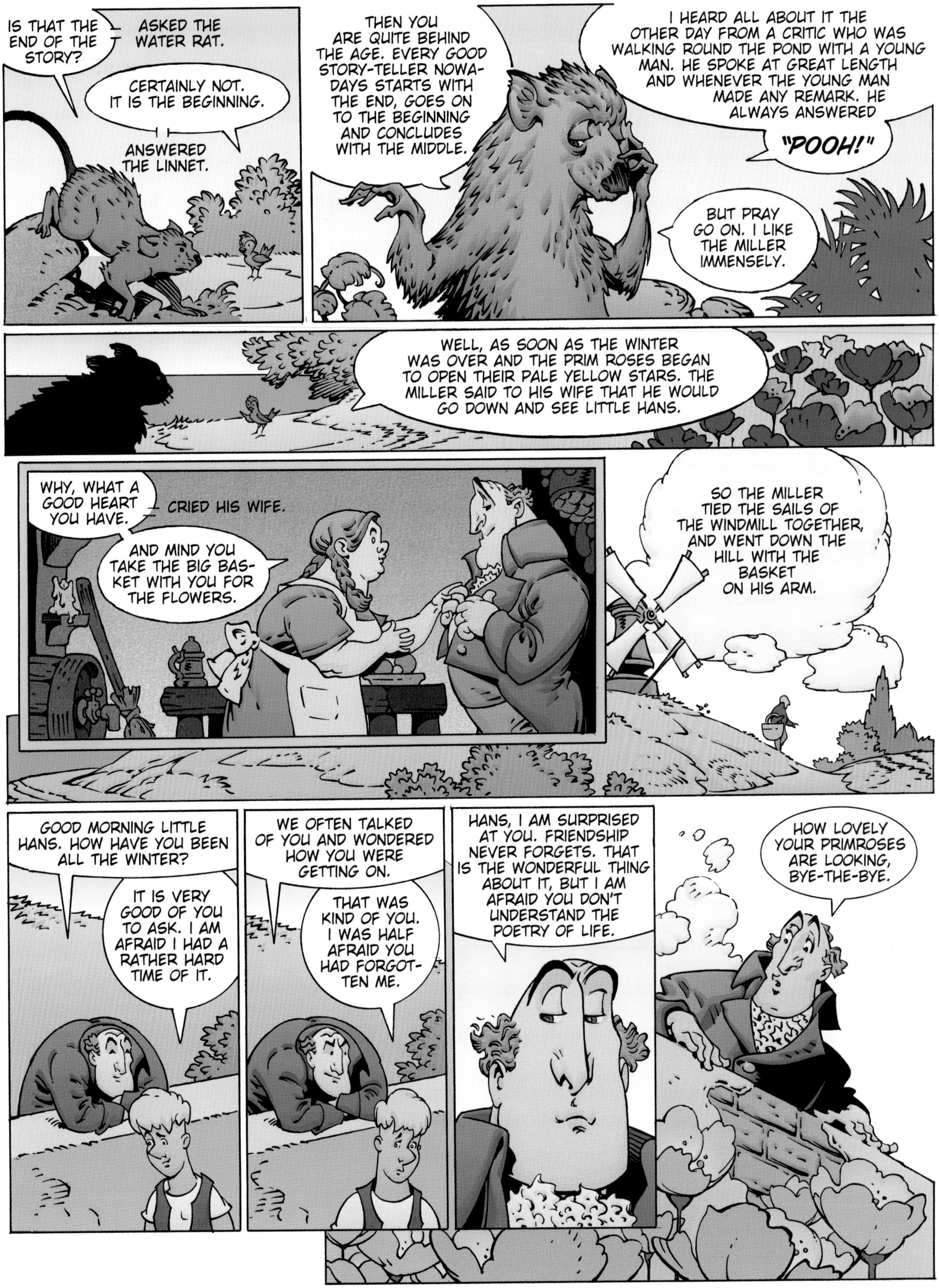

IS THAT THE END OF THE STORY?
ASKED THE WATER RAT.
CERTAINLY NOT. IT IS THE BEGINNING.
ANSWERED THE LINNET.
THEN YOU ARE QUITE BEHIND THE AGE. EVERY GOOD STORY-TELLER NOWADAYS STARTS WITH THE END, GOES ON TO THE BEGINNING AND CONCLUDES WITH THE MIDDLE.
I HEARD ALL ABOUT IT THE OTHER DAY FROM A CRITIC WHO WAS WALKING ROUND THE POND WITH A YOUNG MAN. HE SPOKE AT GREAT LENGTH AND WHENEVER THE YOUNG MAN MADE ANY REMARK. HE ALWAYS ANSWERED
"POOH!"
BUT PRAY GO ON. I LIKE THE MILLER IMMENSELY.
WELL, AS SOON AS THE WINTER WAS OVER AND THE PRIM ROSES BEGAN TO OPEN THEIR PALE YELLOW STARS. THE MILLER SAID TO HIS WIFE THAT HE WOULD GO DOWN AND SEE LITTLE HANS.
WHY, WHAT A GOOD HEART YOU HAVE.
CRIED HIS WIFE.
AND MIND YOU TAKE THE BIG BASKET WITH YOU FOR THE FLOWERS.
SO THE MILLER TIED THE SAILS OF THE WINDMILL TOGETHER, AND WENT DOWN THE HILL WITH THE BASKET ON HIS ARM.
GOOD MORNING LITTLE HANS. HOW HAVE YOU BEEN ALL THE WINTER?
IT IS VERY GOOD OF YOU TO ASK. I AM AFRAID I HAD A RATHER HARD TIME OF IT.
WE OFTEN TALKED OF YOU AND WONDERED HOW YOU WERE GETTING ON.
THAT WAS KIND OF YOU. I WAS HALF AFRAID YOU HAD FORGOTTEN ME.
HANS, I AM SURPRISED AT YOU. FRIENDSHIP NEVER FORGETS. THAT IS THE WONDERFUL THING ABOUT IT, BUT I AM AFRAID YOU DON'T UNDERSTAND THE POETRY OF LIFE.
HOW LOVELY YOUR PRIMROSES ARE LOOKING, BYE-THE-BYE.

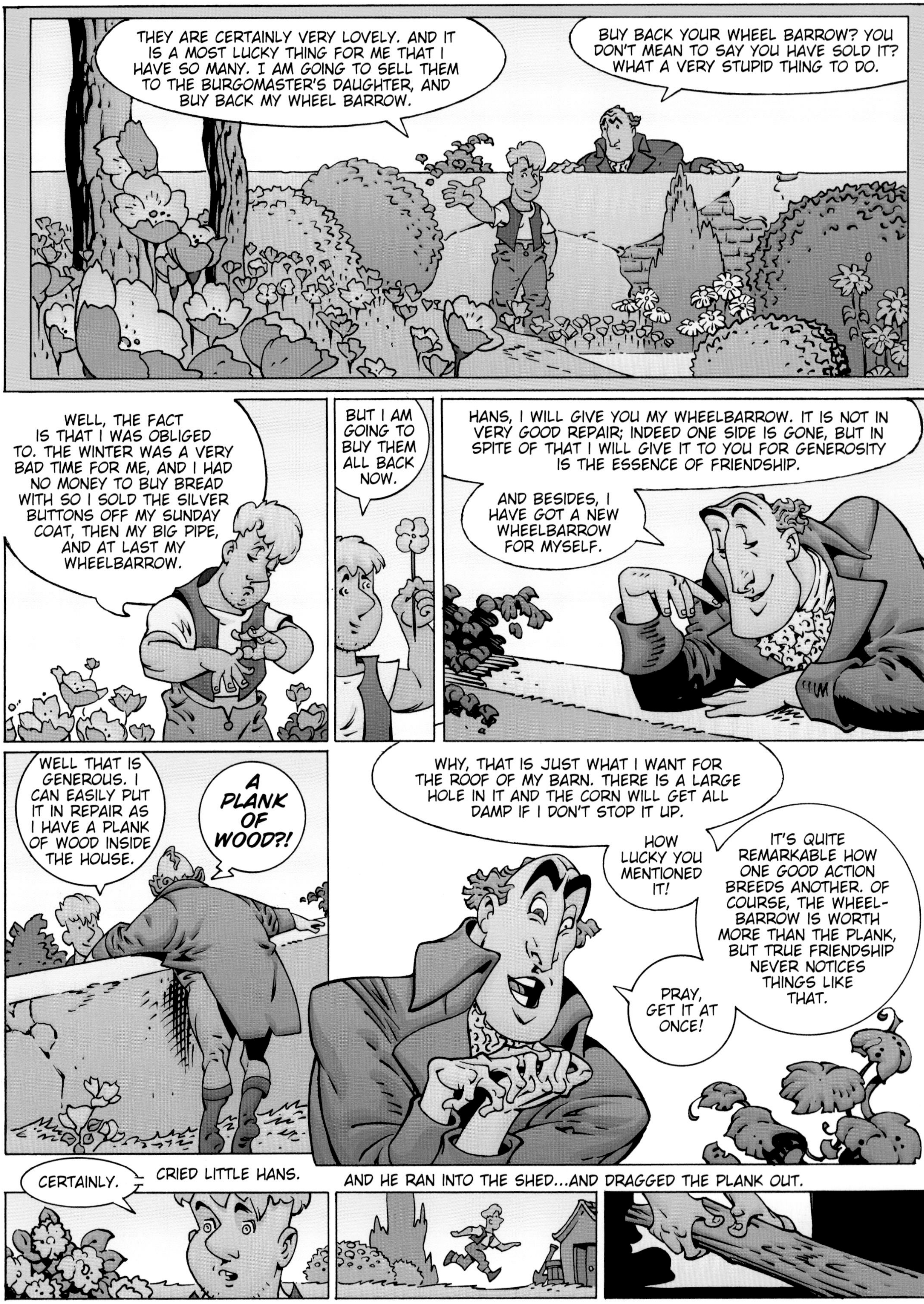
THEY ARE CERTAINLY VERY LOVELY. AND IT IS A MOST LUCKY THING FOR ME THAT I HAVE SO MANY. I AM GOING TO SELL THEM TO THE BURGOMASTER'S DAUGHTER, AND BUY BACK MY WHEEL BARROW.
BUY BACK YOUR WHEEL BARROW? YOU DON'T MEAN TO SAY YOU HAVE SOLD IT? WHAT A VERY STUPID THING TO DO.
WELL, THE FACT IS THAT I WAS OBLIGED TO. THE WINTER WAS A VERY BAD TIME FOR ME, AND I HAD NO MONEY TO BUY BREAD WITH SO I SOLD THE SILVER BUTTONS OFF MY SUNDAY COAT, THEN MY BIG PIPE, AND AT LAST MY WHEELBARROW.
BUT I AM GOING TO BUY THEM ALL BACK NOW.
HANS, I WILL GIVE YOU MY WHEELBARROW. IT IS NOT IN VERY GOOD REPAIR; INDEED ONE SIDE IS GONE, BUT IN SPITE OF THAT I WILL GIVE IT TO YOU FOR GENEROSITY IS THE ESSENCE OF FRIENDSHIP.
AND BESIDES, I HAVE GOT A NEW WHEELBARROW FOR MYSELF.
WELL THAT IS GENEROUS. I CAN EASILY PUT IT IN REPAIR AS I HAVE A PLANK OF WOOD INSIDE THE HOUSE.
A PLANK OF WOOD?!
WHY, THAT IS JUST WHAT I WANT FOR THE ROOF OF MY BARN. THERE IS A LARGE HOLE IN IT AND THE CORN WILL GET ALL DAMP IF I DON'T STOP IT UP.
HOW LUCKY YOU MENTIONED IT!
IT'S QUITE REMARKABLE HOW ONE GOOD ACTION BREEDS ANOTHER. OF COURSE, THE WHEEL-BARROW IS WORTH MORE THAN THE PLANK, BUT TRUE FRIENDSHIP NEVER NOTICES THINGS LIKE THAT.
PRAY, GET IT AT ONCE!
CERTAINLY.
CRIED LITTLE HANS.
AND HE RAN INTO THE SHED...AND DRAGGED THE PLANK OUT.

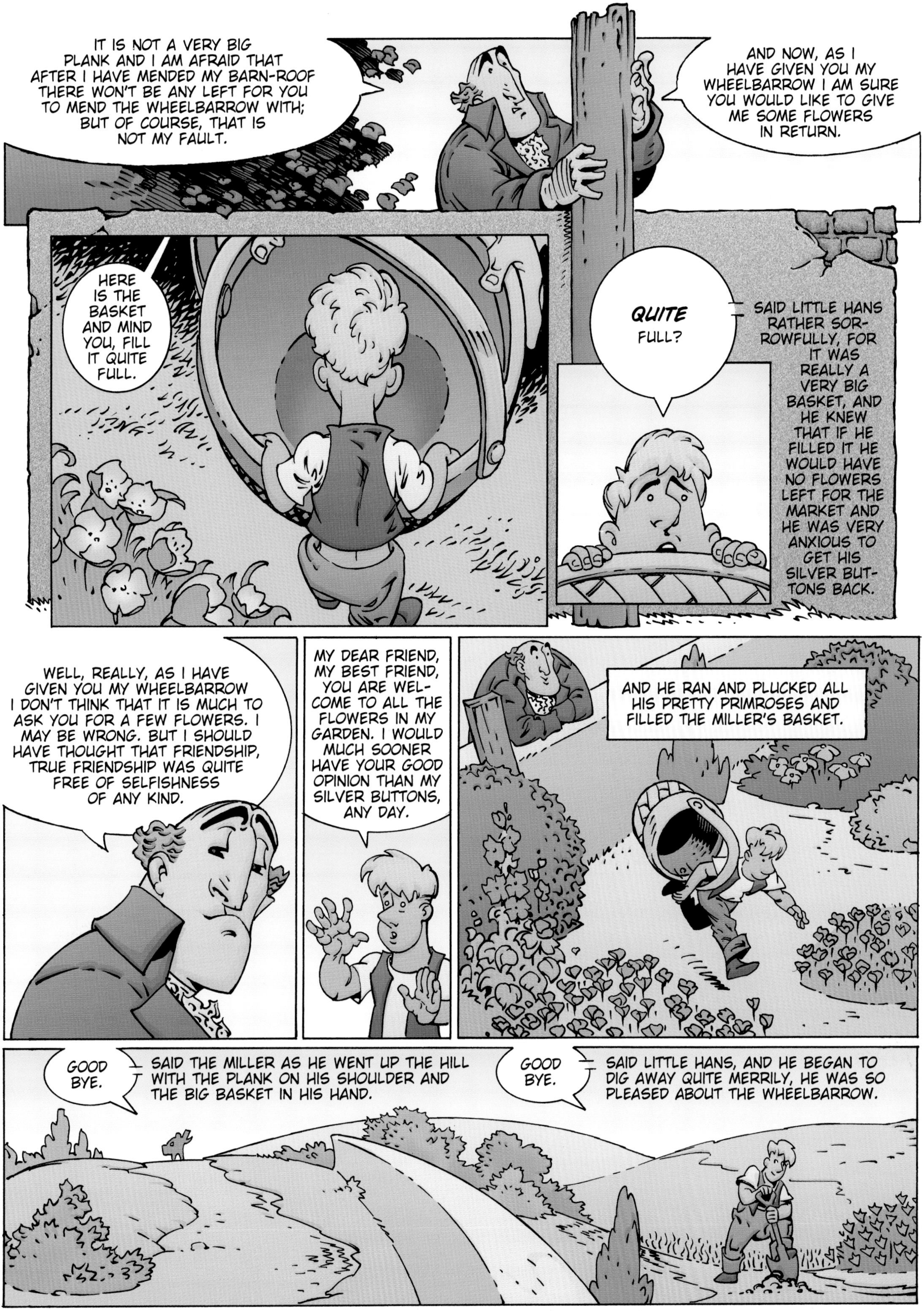

IT IS NOT A VERY BIG PLANK AND I AM AFRAID THAT AFTER I HAVE MENDED MY BARN-ROOF THERE WON'T BE ANY LEFT FOR YOU TO MEND THE WHEELBARROW WITH; BUT OF COURSE, THAT IS NOT MY FAULT.
AND NOW, AS I HAVE GIVEN YOU MY WHEELBARROW I AM SURE YOU WOULD LIKE TO GIVE ME SOME FLOWERS IN RETURN.
HERE IS THE BASKET AND MIND YOU, FILL IT QUITE FULL.
QUITE FULL?
SAID LITTLE HANS RATHER SORROWFULLY, FOR IT WAS REALLY A VERY BIG BASKET, AND HE KNEW THAT IF HE FILLED IT HE WOULD HAVE NO FLOWERS LEFT FOR THE MARKET AND HE WAS VERY ANXIOUS TO GET HIS SILVER BUTTONS BACK.
WELL, REALLY, AS I HAVE GIVEN YOU MY WHEELBARROW I DON'T THINK THAT IT IS MUCH TO ASK YOU FOR A FEW FLOWERS. I MAY BE WRONG. BUT I SHOULD HAVE THOUGHT THAT FRIENDSHIP, TRUE FRIENDSHIP WAS QUITE FREE OF SELFISHNESS OF ANY KIND.
MY DEAR FRIEND, MY BEST FRIEND, YOU ARE WELCOME TO ALL THE FLOWERS IN MY GARDEN. I WOULD MUCH SOONER HAVE YOUR GOOD OPINION THAN MY SILVER BUTTONS, ANY DAY.
AND HE RAN AND PLUCKED ALL HIS PRETTY PRIMROSES AND FILLED THE MILLER'S BASKET.
GOOD BYE.
SAID THE MILLER AS HE WENT UP THE HILL WITH THE PLANK ON HIS SHOULDER AND THE BIG BASKET IN HIS HAND.
GOOD BYE.
SAID LITTLE HANS, AND HE BEGAN TO DIG AWAY QUITE MERRILY, HE WAS SO PLEASED ABOUT THE WHEELBARROW.

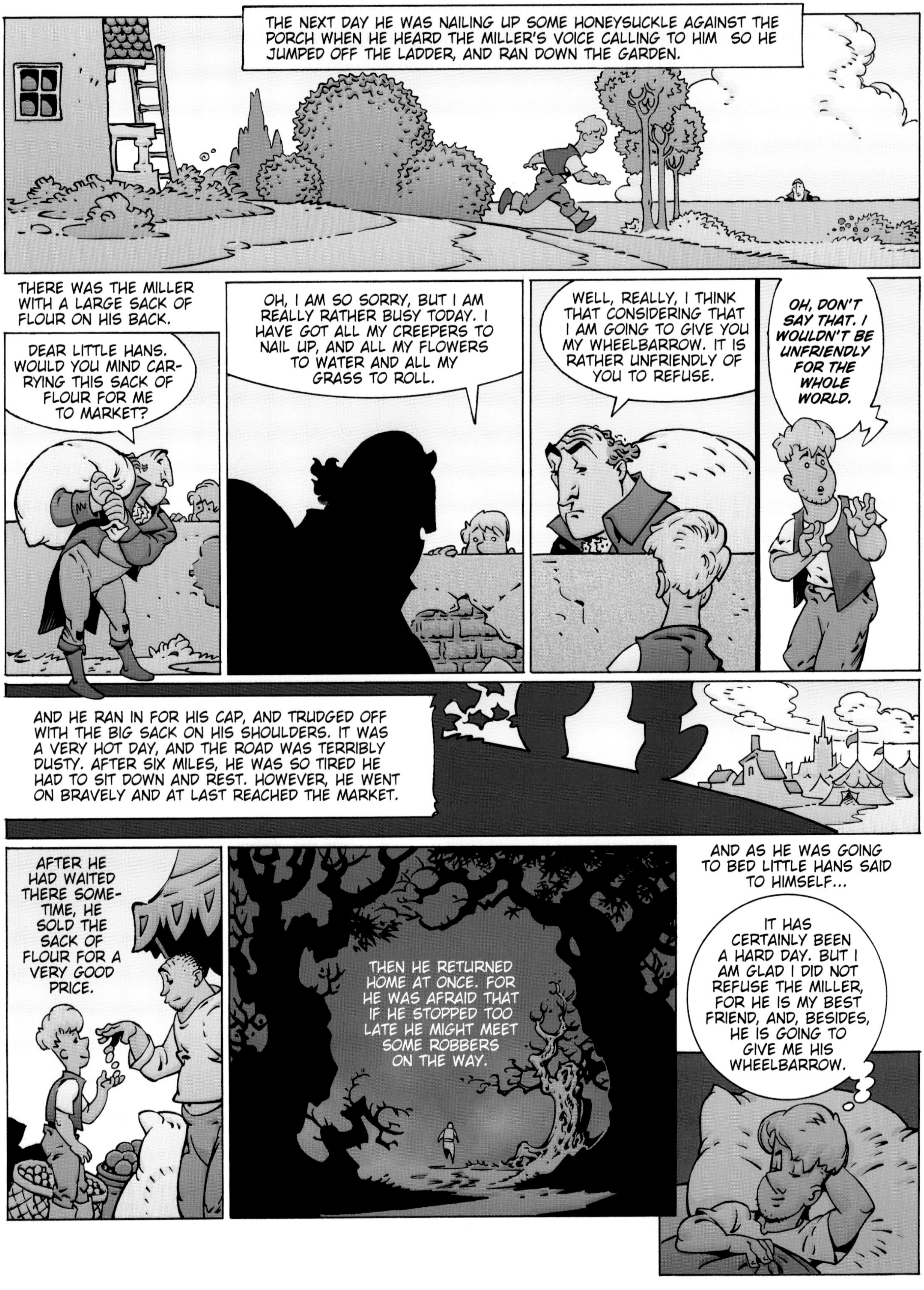
THE NEXT DAY HE WAS NAILING UP SOME HONEYSUCKLE AGAINST THE PORCH WHEN HE HEARD THE MILLER'S VOICE CALLING TO HIM SO HE JUMPED OFF THE LADDER, AND RAN DOWN THE GARDEN.
THERE WAS THE MILLER WITH A LARGE SACK OF FLOUR ON HIS BACK.
DEAR LITTLE HANS. WOULD YOU MIND CARRYING THIS SACK OF FLOUR FOR ME TO MARKET?
OH, I AM SO SORRY, BUT I AM REALLY RATHER BUSY TODAY. I HAVE GOT ALL MY CREEPERS TO NAIL UP, AND ALL MY FLOWERS TO WATER AND ALL MY GRASS TO ROLL.
WELL, REALLY, I THINK THAT CONSIDERING THAT I AM GOING TO GIVE YOU MY WHEELBARROW. IT IS RATHER UNFRIENDLY OF YOU TO REFUSE.
OH, DON'T SAY THAT. I WOULDN'T BE UNFRIENDLY FOR THE WHOLE WORLD.
AND HE RAN IN FOR HIS CAP, AND TRUDGED OFF WITH THE BIG SACK ON HIS SHOULDERS. IT WAS A VERY HOT DAY, AND THE ROAD WAS TERRIBLY DUSTY. AFTER SIX MILES, HE WAS SO TIRED HE HAD TO SIT DOWN AND REST. HOWEVER, HE WENT ON BRAVELY AND AT LAST REACHED THE MARKET.
AFTER HE HAD WAITED THERE SOMETIME, HE SOLD THE SACK OF FLOUR FOR A VERY GOOD PRICE.
THEN HE RETURNED HOME AT ONCE. FOR HE WAS AFRAID THAT IF HE STOPPED TOO LATE HE MIGHT MEET SOME ROBBERS ON THE WAY.
AND AS HE WAS GOING TO BED LITTLE HANS SAID TO HIMSELF...
IT HAS CERTAINLY BEEN A HARD DAY. BUT I AM GLAD I DID NOT REFUSE THE MILLER, FOR HE IS MY BEST FRIEND, AND, BESIDES, HE IS GOING TO GIVE ME HIS WHEELBARROW.

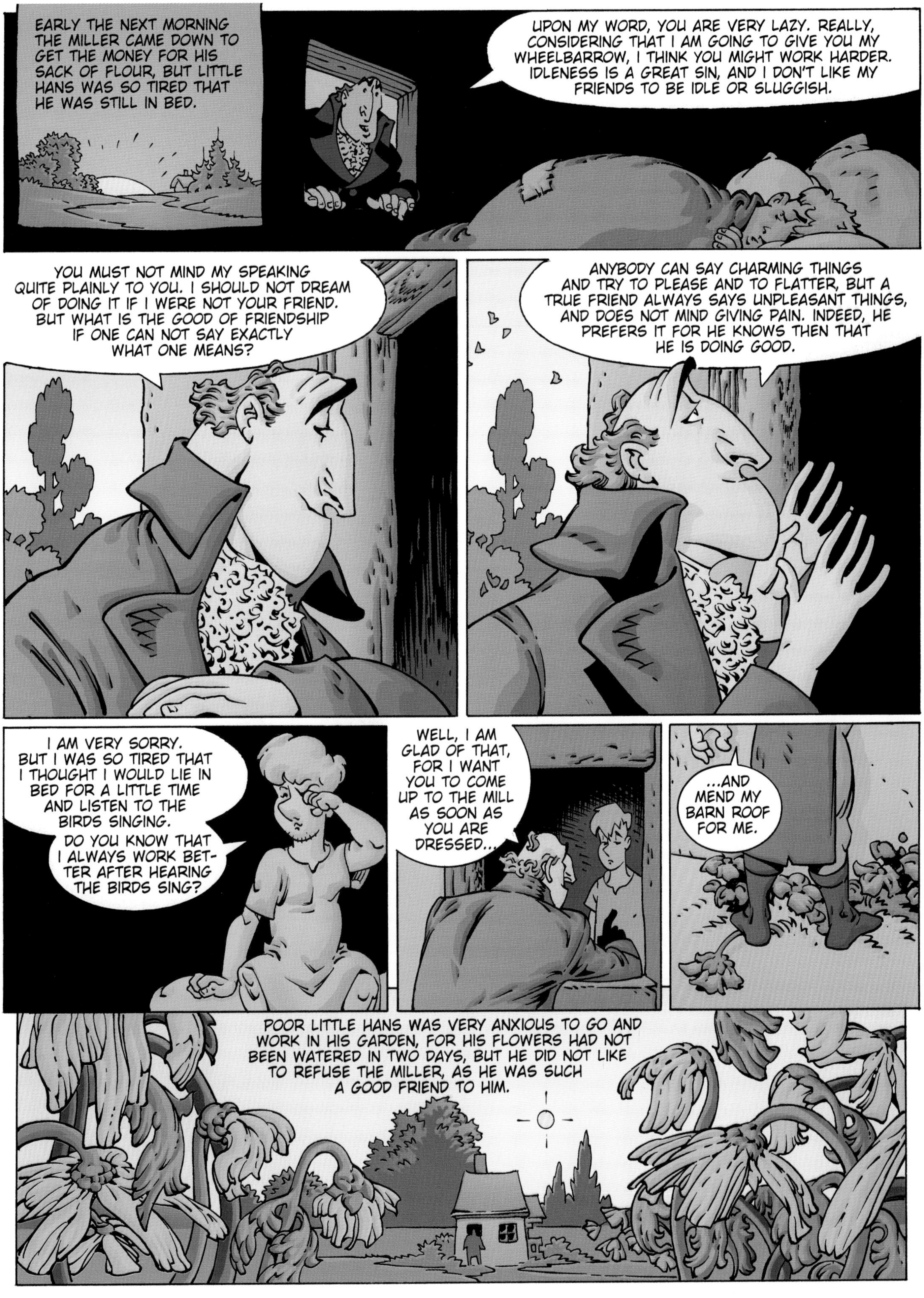
EARLY THE NEXT MORNING THE MILLER CAME DOWN TO GET THE MONEY FOR HIS SACK OF FLOUR, BUT LITTLE HANS WAS SO TIRED THAT HE WAS STILL IN BED.
UPON MY WORD, YOU ARE VERY LAZY. REALLY, CONSIDERING THAT I AM GOING TO GIVE YOU MY WHEELBARROW, I THINK YOU MIGHT WORK HARDER. IDLENESS IS A GREAT SIN, AND I DON'T LIKE MY FRIENDS TO BE IDLE OR SLUGGISH.
YOU MUST NOT MIND MY SPEAKING QUITE PLAINLY TO YOU. I SHOULD NOT DREAM OF DOING IT IF I WERE NOT YOUR FRIEND. BUT WHAT IS THE GOOD OF FRIENDSHIP IF ONE CAN NOT SAY EXACTLY WHAT ONE MEANS?
ANYBODY CAN SAY CHARMING THINGS AND TRY TO PLEASE AND TO FLATTER, BUT A TRUE FRIEND ALWAYS SAYS UNPLEASANT THINGS, AND DOES NOT MIND GIVING PAIN. INDEED, HE PREFERS IT FOR HE KNOWS THEN THAT HE IS DOING GOOD.
I AM VERY SORRY. BUT I WAS SO TIRED THAT I THOUGHT I WOULD LIE IN BED FOR A LITTLE TIME AND LISTEN TO THE BIRDS SINGING.
DO YOU KNOW THAT I ALWAYS WORK BETTER AFTER HEARING THE BIRDS SING?
WELL, I AM GLAD OF THAT, FOR I WANT YOU TO COME UP TO THE MILL AS SOON AS YOU ARE DRESSED...
...AND MEND MY BARN ROOF FOR ME.
POOR LITTLE HANS WAS VERY ANXIOUS TO GO AND WORK IN HIS GARDEN, FOR HIS FLOWERS HAD NOT BEEN WATERED IN TWO DAYS, BUT HE DID NOT LIKE TO REFUSE THE MILLER, AS HE WAS SUCH A GOOD FRIEND TO HIM.

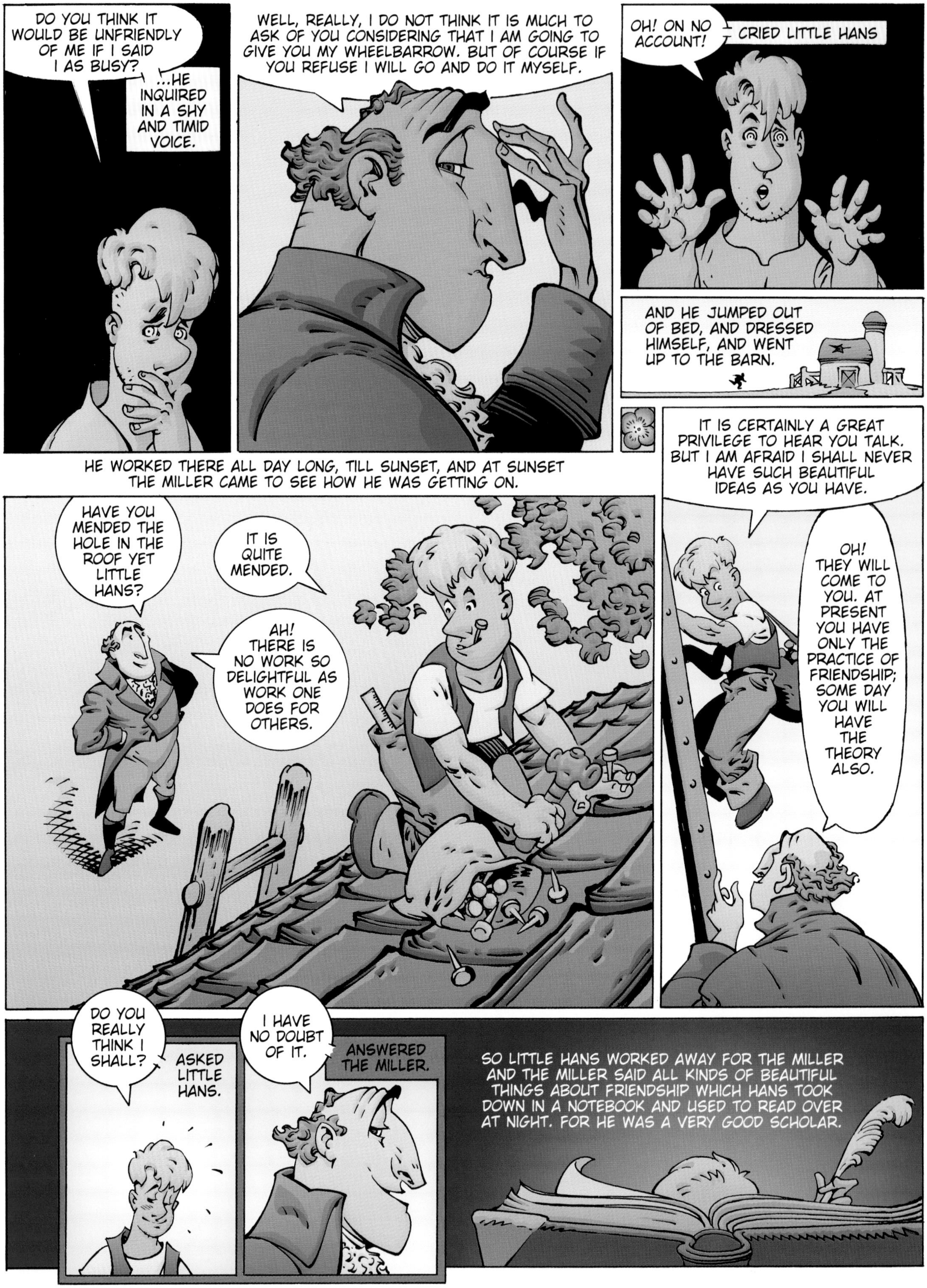

DO YOU THINK IT WOULD BE UNFRIENDLY OF ME IF I SAID I AS BUSY?
...HE INQUIRED IN A SHY AND TIMID VOICE.
WELL, REALLY, I DO NOT THINK IT IS MUCH TO ASK OF YOU CONSIDERING THAT I AM GOING TO GIVE YOU MY WHEELBARROW. BUT OF COURSE IF YOU REFUSE I WILL GO AND DO IT MYSELF.
OH! ON NO ACCOUNT!
CRIED LITTLE HANS
AND HE JUMPED OUT OF BED, AND DRESSED HIMSELF, AND WENT UP TO THE BARN.
HE WORKED THERE ALL DAY LONG, TILL SUNSET, AND AT SUNSET THE MILLER CAME TO SEE HOW HE WAS GETTING ON.
HAVE YOU MENDED THE HOLE IN THE ROOF YET LITTLE HANS?
IT IS QUITE MENDED.
AH! THERE IS NO WORK SO DELIGHTFUL AS WORK ONE DOES FOR OTHERS.
IT IS CERTAINLY A GREAT PRIVILEGE TO HEAR YOU TALK. BUT I AM AFRAID I SHALL NEVER HAVE SUCH BEAUTIFUL IDEAS AS YOU HAVE.
OH! THEY WILL COME TO YOU. AT PRESENT YOU HAVE ONLY THE PRACTICE OF FRIENDSHIP; SOME DAY YOU WILL HAVE THE THEORY ALSO.
DO YOU REALLY THINK I SHALL?
ASKED LITTLE HANS.
I HAVE NO DOUBT OF IT.
ANSWERED THE MILLER.
SO LITTLE HANS WORKED AWAY FOR THE MILLER AND THE MILLER SAID ALL KINDS OF BEAUTIFUL THINGS ABOUT FRIENDSHIP WHICH HANS TOOK DOWN IN A NOTEBOOK AND USED TO READ OVER AT NIGHT. FOR HE WAS A VERY GOOD SCHOLAR.

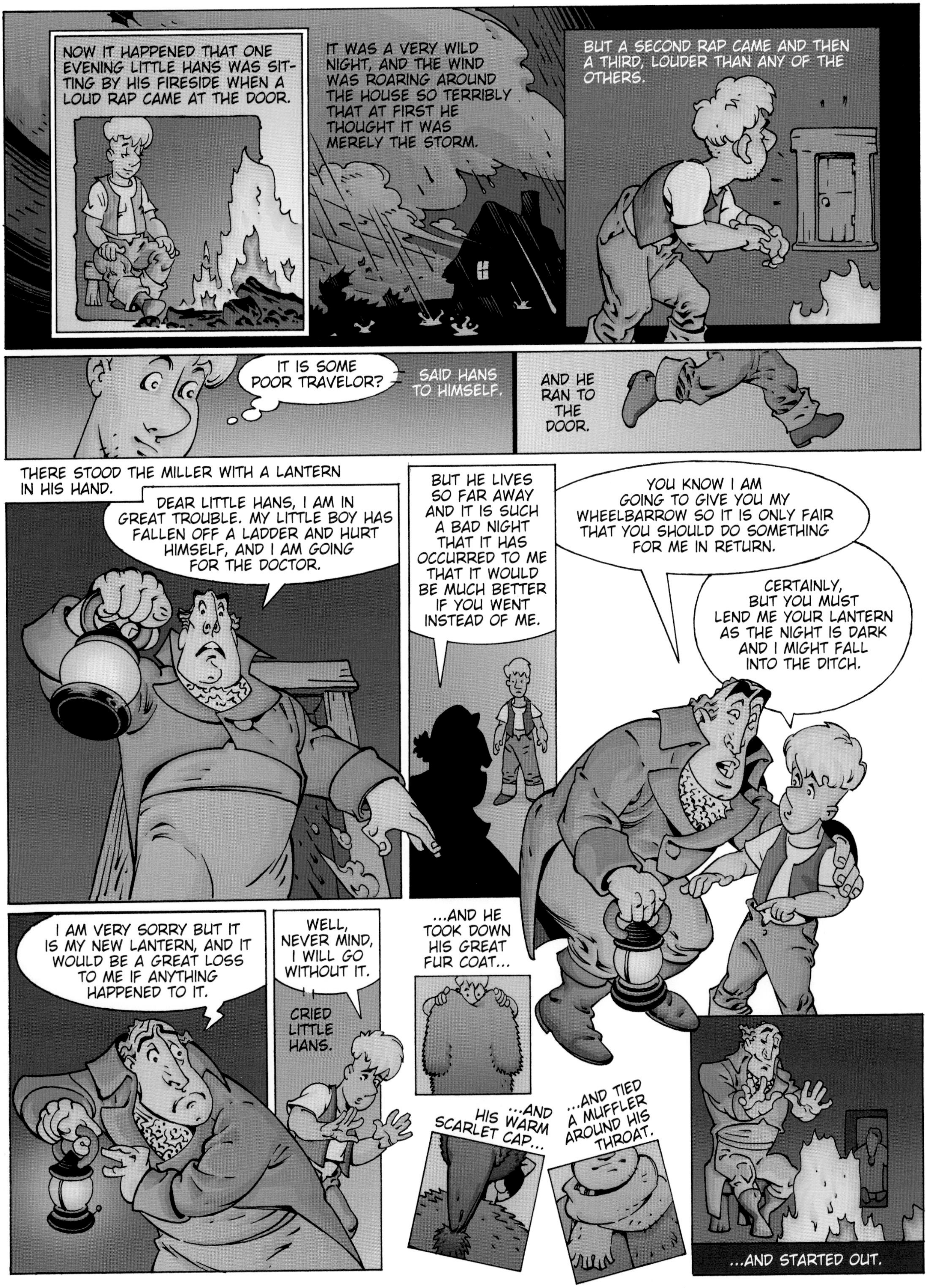
NOW IT HAPPENED THAT ONE EVENING LITTLE HANS WAS SITTING BY HIS FIRESIDE WHEN A LOUD RAP CAME AT THE DOOR.
IT WAS A VERY WILD NIGHT, AND THE WIND WAS ROARING AROUND THE HOUSE SO TERRIBLY THAT AT FIRST HE THOUGHT IT WAS MERELY THE STORM.
BUT A SECOND RAP CAME AND THEN A THIRD, LOUDER THAN ANY OF THE OTHERS.
IT IS SOME POOR TRAVELOR?
SAID HANS TO HIMSELF.
AND HE RAN TO THE DOOR.
THERE STOOD THE MILLER WITH A LANTERN IN HIS HAND.
DEAR LITTLE HANS, I AM IN GREAT TROUBLE. MY LITTLE BOY HAS FALLEN OFF A LADDER AND HURT HIMSELF, AND I AM GOING FOR THE DOCTOR.
BUT HE LIVES SO FAR AWAY AND IT IS SUCH A BAD NIGHT THAT IT HAS OCCURRED TO ME THAT IT WOULD BE MUCH BETTER IF YOU WENT INSTEAD OF ME.
YOU KNOW I AM GOING TO GIVE YOU MY WHEELBARROW SO IT IS ONLY FAIR THAT YOU SHOULD DO SOMETHING FOR ME IN RETURN.
CERTAINLY, BUT YOU MUST LEND ME YOUR LANTERN AS THE NIGHT IS DARK AND I MIGHT FALL INTO THE DITCH.
I AM VERY SORRY BUT IT IS MY NEW LANTERN, AND IT WOULD BE A GREAT LOSS TO ME IF ANYTHING HAPPENED TO IT.
WELL, NEVER MIND, I WILL GO WITHOUT IT.
CRIED LITTLE HANS.
...AND HE TOOK DOWN HIS GREAT FUR COAT...
...AND HIS WARM SCARLET CAP...
...AND TIED A MUFFLER AROUND HIS THROAT.
...AND STARTED OUT.

WHAT A DREADFUL STORM IT WAS! THE NIGHT WAS SO BLACK THAT LITTLE HANS COULD HARDLY SEE, AND THE WIND WAS SO STRONG THAT HE COULD SCARCELY STAND.
HOWEVER HE WAS VERY COURAGEOUS AND AFTER HE HAD BEEN WALKING ABOUT THREE HOURS, HE ARRIVED AT THE DOCTOR'S HOUSE AND KNOCKED AT THE DOOR.
WHO IS THERE?
LITTLE HANS, DOCTOR.
WHAT DO YOU WANT, LITTLE HANS?
THE MILLER'S SON HAS FALLEN FROM A LADDER AND THE MILLER WANTS YOU TO COME AT ONCE.
ALL RIGHT.
SAID THE DOCTOR..
AND HE ORDERED HIS HORSE AND HIS BIG BOOTS, AND HIS LANTERN, AND CAME DOWNSTAIRS, AND RODE OFF IN THE DIRECTION OF THE MILLER'S HOUSE, LITTLE HANS TRUDGING BEHIND HIM.
BUT THE STORM GREW WORSE AND WORSE, AND THE RAIN FELL IN TORENTS, AND LITTLE HANS COULD NOT SEE WHERE HE WAS GOING OR KEEP UP WITH THE HORSE.
AT LAST HE LOST HIS WAY AND WANDERED OFF ON THE MOOR WHICH WAS A VERY DANGEROUS PLACE AS IT WAS FULL OF DEEP HOLES...AND THERE POOR LITTLE HANS WAS DROWNED.

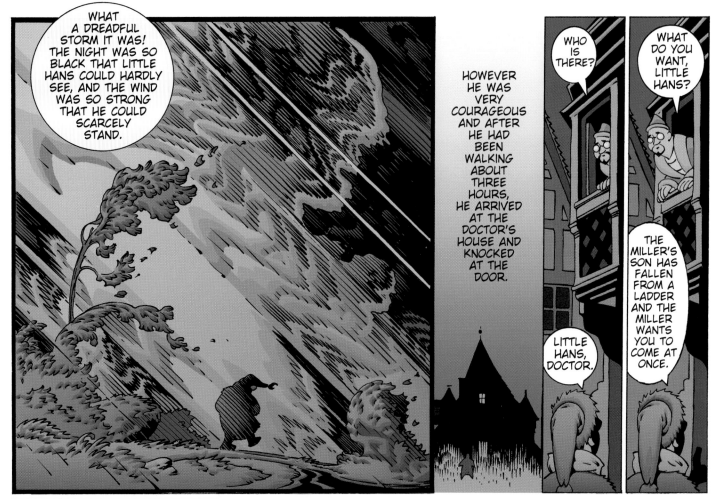

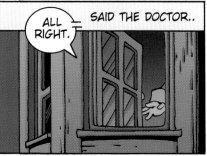

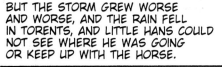

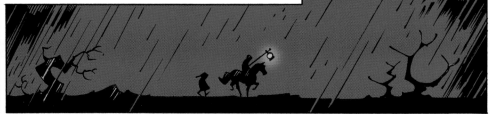

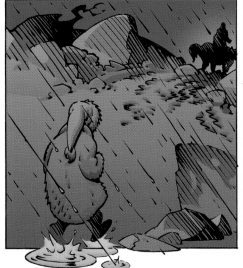

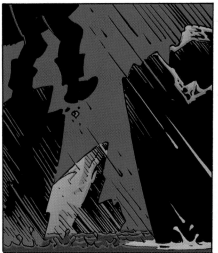

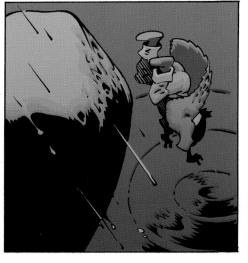

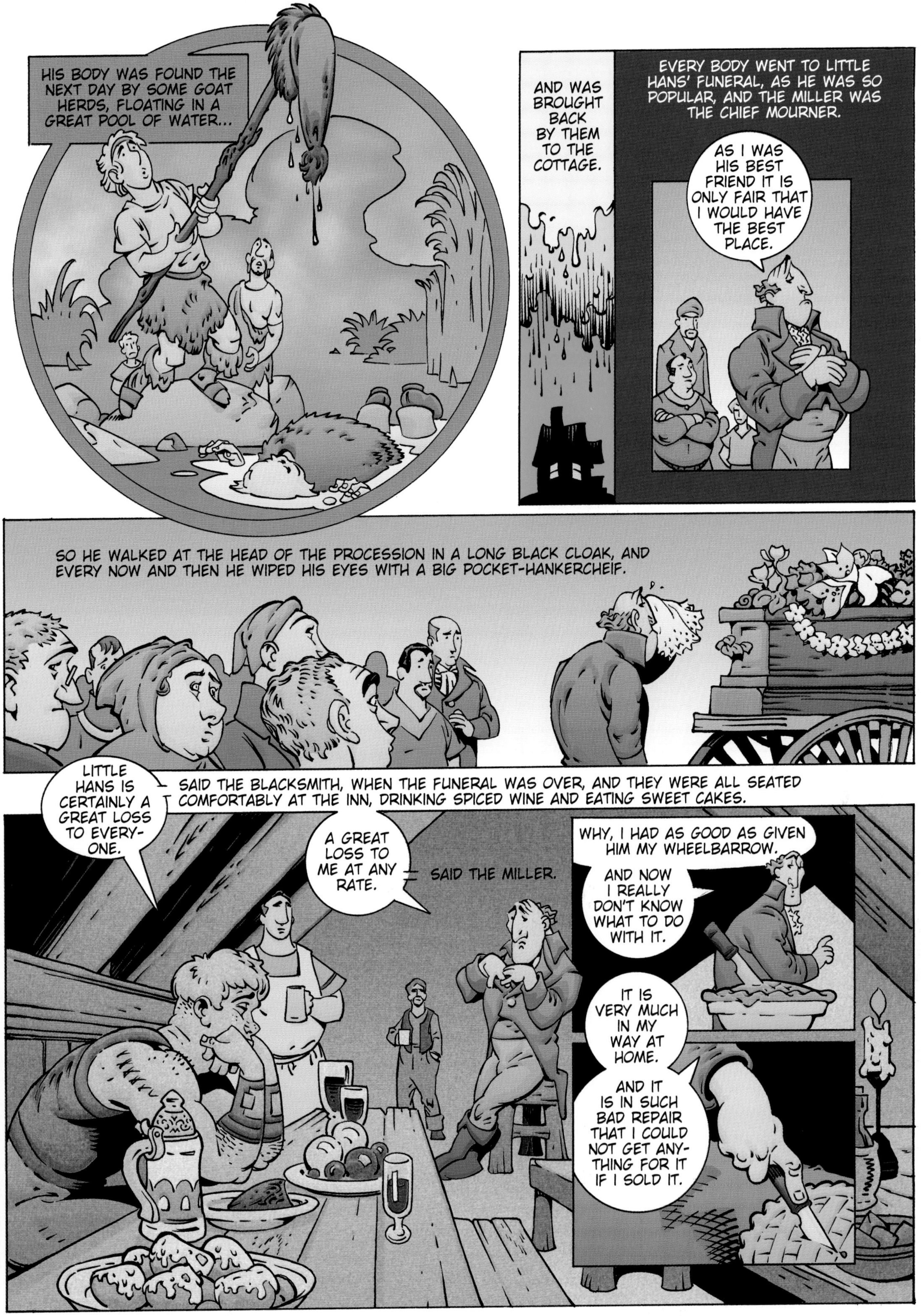

HIS BODY WAS FOUND THE NEXT DAY BY SOME GOAT HERDS, FLOATING IN A GREAT POOL OF WATER...
AND WAS BROUGHT BACK BY THEM TO THE COTTAGE.
EVERY BODY WENT TO LITTLE HANS' FUNERAL, AS HE WAS SO POPULAR, AND THE MILLER WAS THE CHIEF MOURNER.
AS I WAS HIS BEST FRIEND IT IS ONLY FAIR THAT I WOULD HAVE THE BEST PLACE.
SO HE WALKED AT THE HEAD OF THE PROCESSION IN A LONG BLACK CLOAK, AND EVERY NOW AND THEN HE WIPED HIS EYES WITH A BIG POCKET-HANKERCHEIF.
LITTLE HANS IS CERTAINLY A GREAT LOSS TO EVERY-ONE.
SAID THE BLACKSMITH, WHEN THE FUNERAL WAS OVER, AND THEY WERE ALL SEATED COMFORTABLY AT THE INN, DRINKING SPICED WINE AND EATING SWEET CAKES.
A GREAT LOSS TO ME AT ANY RATE.
SAID THE MILLER.
WHY, I HAD AS GOOD AS GIVEN HIM MY WHEELBARROW.
AND NOW I REALLY DON'T KNOW WHAT TO DO WITH IT.
IT IS VERY MUCH IN MY WAY AT HOME.
AND IT IS IN SUCH BAD REPAIR THAT I COULD NOT GET ANY-THING FOR IT IF I SOLD IT.

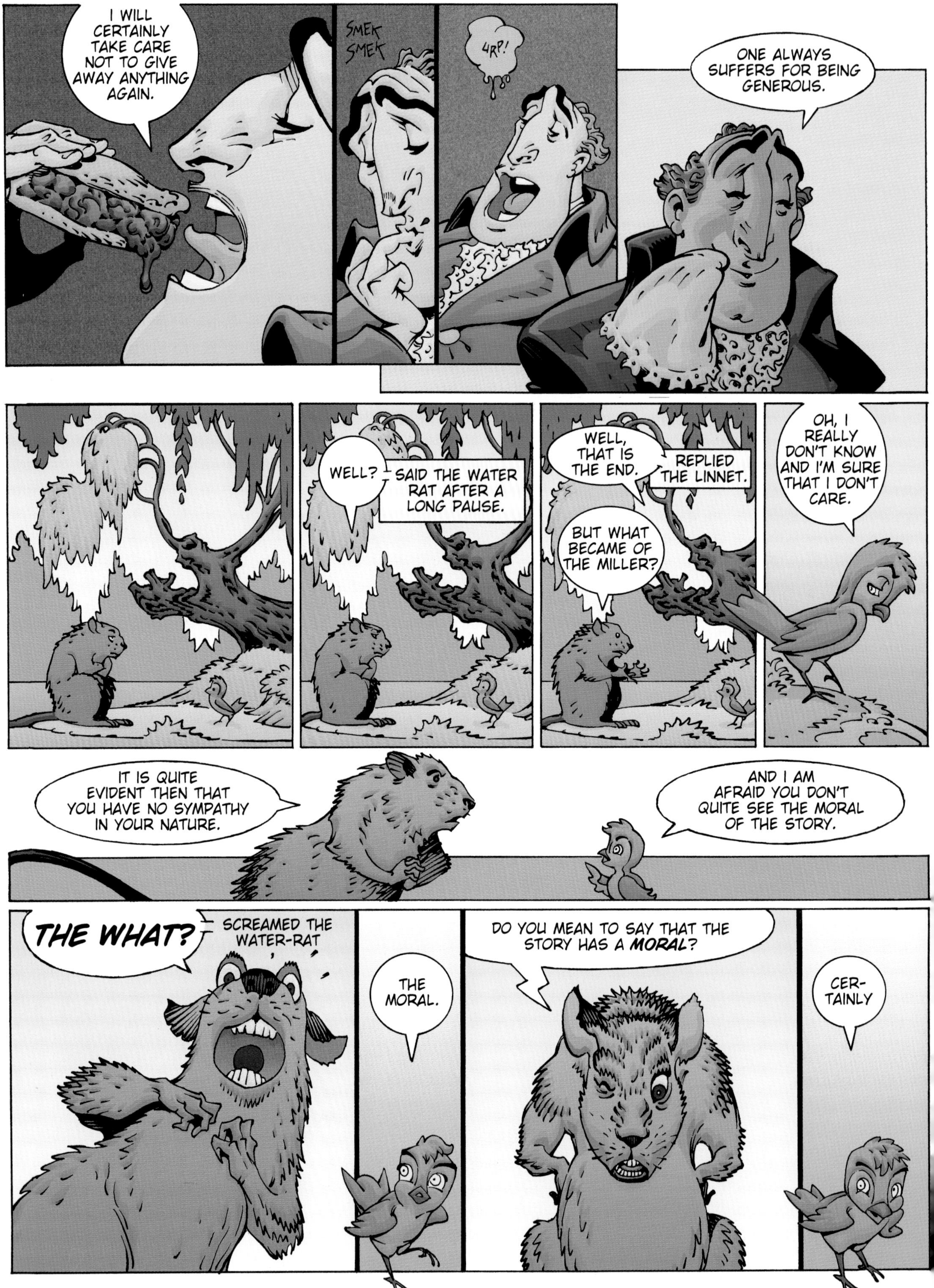

I WILL CERTAINLY TAKE CARE NOT TO GIVE AWAY ANYTHING AGAIN.
SMEK SMEK
URP!
ONE ALWAYS SUFFERS FOR BEING GENEROUS.
WELL?
SAID THE WATER RAT AFTER A LONG PAUSE.
WELL, THAT IS THE END.
REPLIED THE LINNET.
BUT WHAT BECAME OF THE MILLER?
OH, I REALLY DON'T KNOW AND I'M SURE THAT I DON'T CARE.
IT IS QUITE EVIDENT THEN THAT YOU HAVE NO SYMPATHY IN YOUR NATURE.
AND I AM AFRAID YOU DON'T QUITE SEE THE MORAL OF THE STORY.
THE WHAT?
SCREAMED THE WATER-RAT
THE MORAL.
DO YOU MEAN TO SAY THAT THE STORY HAS A MORAL?
CER-TAINLY

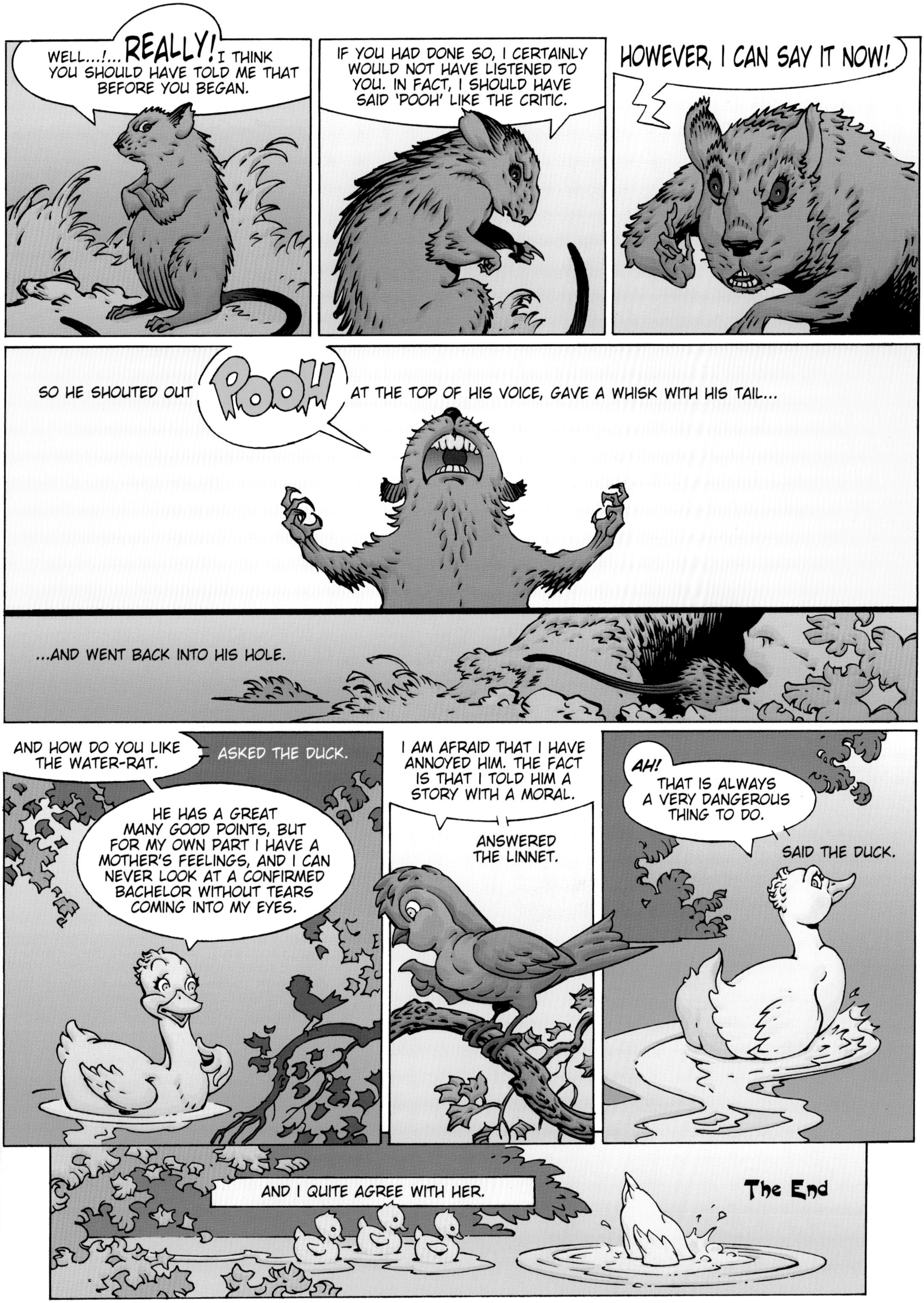
WELL...!...REALLY! I THINK YOU SHOULD HAVE TOLD ME THAT BEFORE YOU BEGAN.
IF YOU HAD DONE SO, I CERTAINLY WOULD NOT HAVE LISTENED TO YOU. IN FACT, I SHOULD HAVE SAID 'POOH' LIKE THE CRITIC.
HOWEVER, I CAN SAY IT NOW!
SO HE SHOUTED OUT
POOH
AT THE TOP OF HIS VOICE, GAVE A WHISK WITH HIS TAIL...
...AND WENT BACK INTO HIS HOLE.
AND HOW DO YOU LIKE THE WATER-RAT.
ASKED THE DUCK.
HE HAS A GREAT MANY GOOD POINTS, BUT FOR MY OWN PART I HAVE A MOTHER'S FEELINGS, AND I CAN NEVER LOOK AT A CONFIRMED BACHELOR WITHOUT TEARS COMING INTO MY EYES.
I AM AFRAID THAT I HAVE ANNOYED HIM. THE FACT IS THAT I TOLD HIM A STORY WITH A MORAL.
ANSWERED THE LINNET.
AH!
THAT IS ALWAYS A VERY DANGEROUS THING TO DO.
SAID THE DUCK.
AND I QUITE AGREE WITH HER.
The End

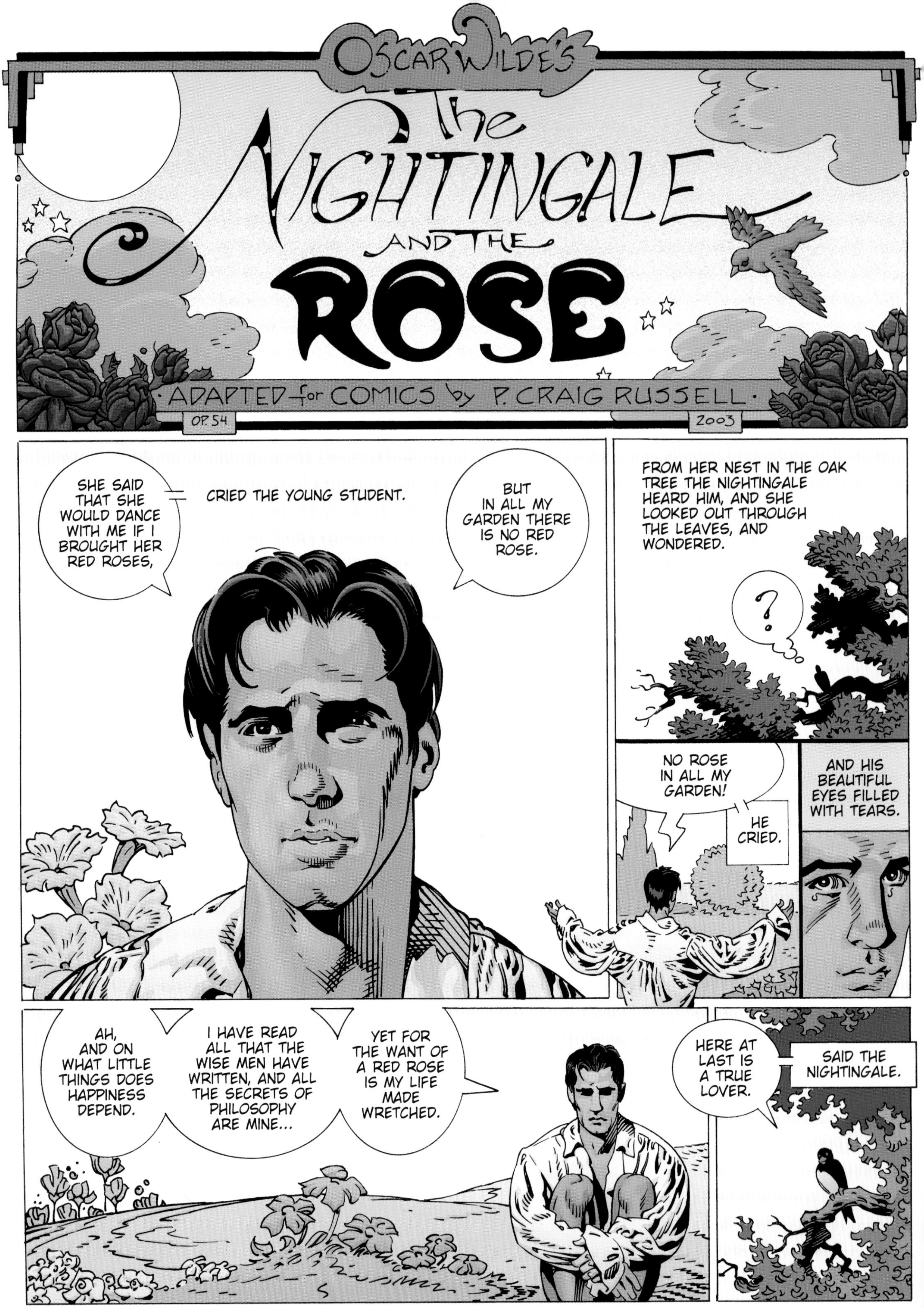
OSCAR WILDE'S
The NIGHTINGALE AND THE ROSE
·ADAPTED for COMICS by P. CRAIG RUSSELL·
OP. 54
2003
SHE SAID THAT SHE WOULD DANCE WITH ME IF I BROUGHT HER RED ROSES,
CRIED THE YOUNG STUDENT.
BUT IN ALL MY GARDEN THERE IS NO RED ROSE.
FROM HER NEST IN THE OAK TREE THE NIGHTINGALE HEARD HIM, AND SHE LOOKED OUT THROUGH THE LEAVES, AND WONDERED.
?
NO ROSE IN ALL MY GARDEN!
HE CRIED.
AND HIS BEAUTIFUL EYES FILLED WITH TEARS.
AH, AND ON WHAT LITTLE THINGS DOES HAPPINESS DEPEND.
I HAVE READ ALL THAT THE WISE MEN HAVE WRITTEN, AND ALL THE SECRETS OF PHILOSOPHY ARE MINE...
YET FOR THE WANT OF A RED ROSE IS MY LIFE MADE WRETCHED.
HERE AT LAST IS A TRUE LOVER.
SAID THE NIGHTINGALE.

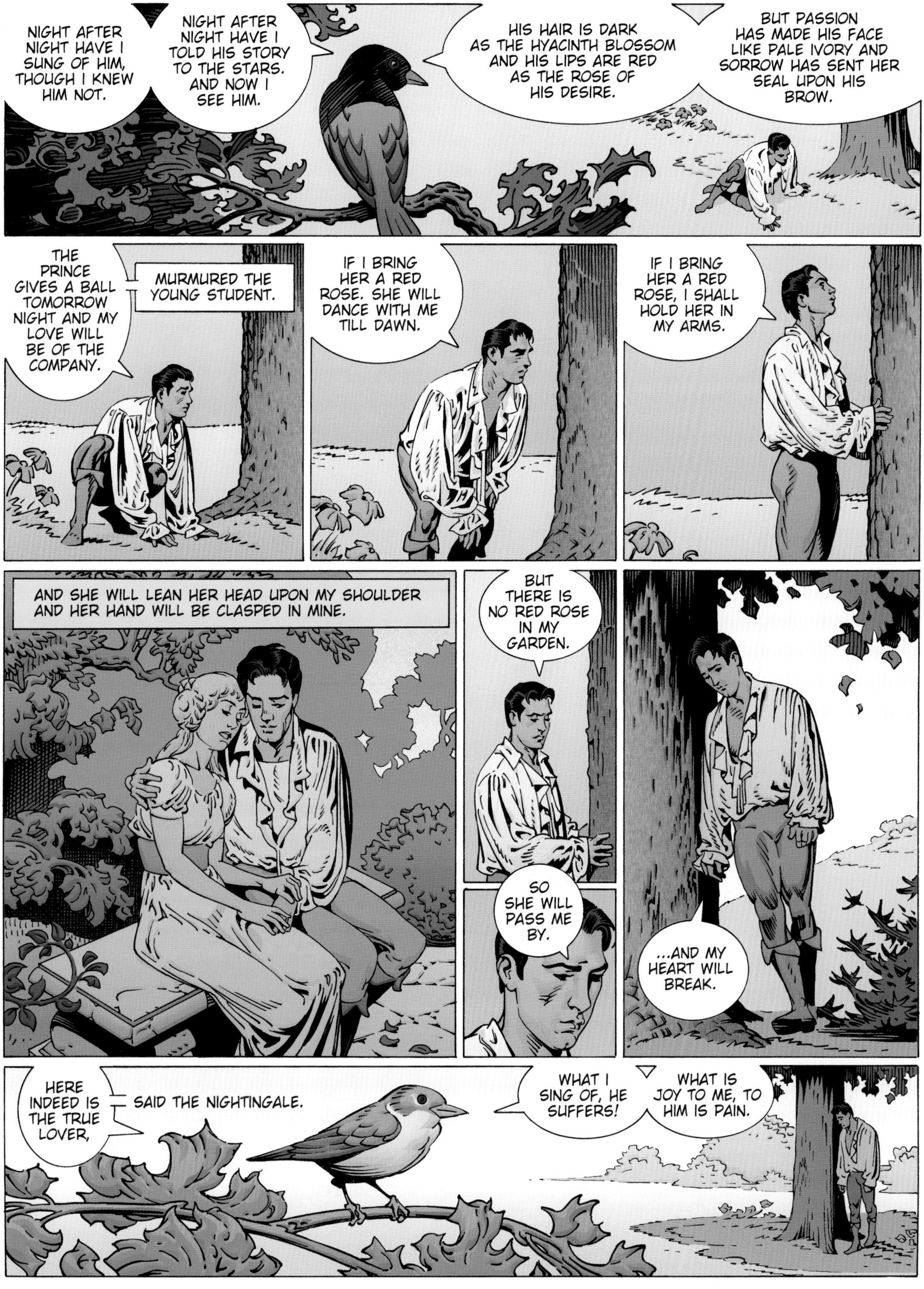

NIGHT AFTER NIGHT HAVE I SUNG OF HIM, THOUGH I KNEW HIM NOT.
NIGHT AFTER NIGHT HAVE I TOLD HIS STORY TO THE STARS. AND NOW I SEE HIM.
HIS HAIR IS DARK AS THE HYACINTH BLOSSOM AND HIS LIPS ARE RED AS THE ROSE OF HIS DESIRE.
BUT PASSION HAS MADE HIS FACE LIKE PALE IVORY AND SORROW HAS SENT HER SEAL UPON HIS BROW.
THE PRINCE GIVES A BALL TOMORROW NIGHT AND MY LOVE WILL BE OF THE COMPANY.
MURMURED THE YOUNG STUDENT.
IF I BRING HER A RED ROSE. SHE WILL DANCE WITH ME TILL DAWN.
IF I BRING HER A RED ROSE, I SHALL HOLD HER IN MY ARMS.
AND SHE WILL LEAN HER HEAD UPON MY SHOULDER AND HER HAND WILL BE CLASPED IN MINE.
BUT THERE IS NO RED ROSE IN MY GARDEN.
SO SHE WILL PASS ME BY.
...AND MY HEART WILL BREAK.
HERE INDEED IS THE TRUE LOVER,
SAID THE NIGHTINGALE.
WHAT I SING OF, HE SUFFERS!
WHAT IS JOY TO ME, TO HIM IS PAIN.

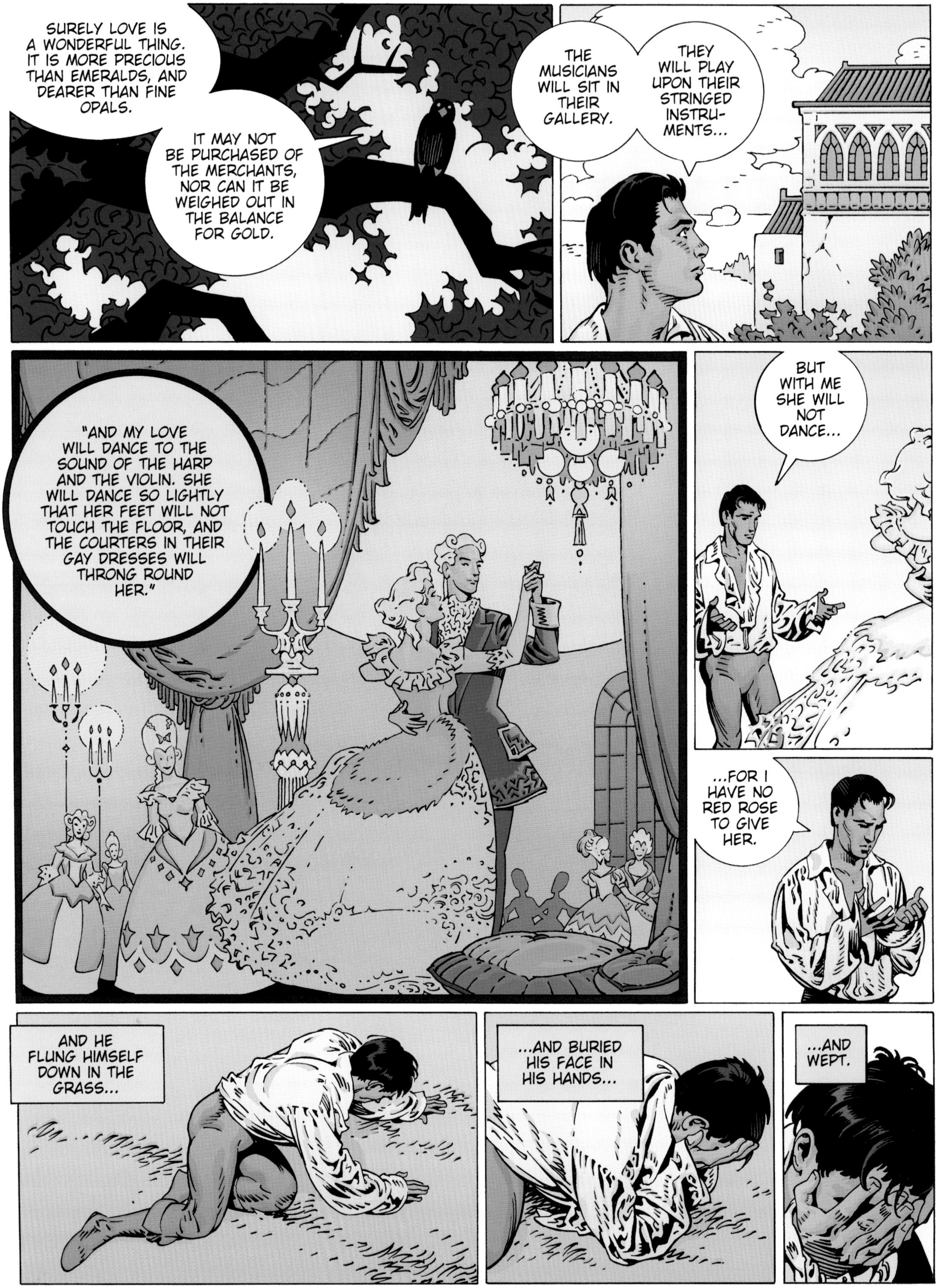
SURELY LOVE IS A WONDERFUL THING. IT IS MORE PRECIOUS THAN EMERALDS, AND DEARER THAN FINE OPALS.
IT MAY NOT BE PURCHASED OF THE MERCHANTS, NOR CAN IT BE WEIGHED OUT IN THE BALANCE FOR GOLD.
THE MUSICIANS WILL SIT IN THEIR GALLERY.
THEY WILL PLAY UPON THEIR STRINGED INSTRU-MENTS...
"AND MY LOVE WILL DANCE TO THE SOUND OF THE HARP AND THE VIOLIN. SHE WILL DANCE SO LIGHTLY THAT HER FEET WILL NOT TOUCH THE FLOOR, AND THE COURTERS IN THEIR GAY DRESSES WILL THRONG ROUND HER."
BUT WITH ME SHE WILL NOT DANCE...
...FOR I HAVE NO RED ROSE TO GIVE HER.
AND HE FLUNG HIMSELF DOWN IN THE GRASS...
...AND BURIED HIS FACE IN HIS HANDS...
...AND WEPT.

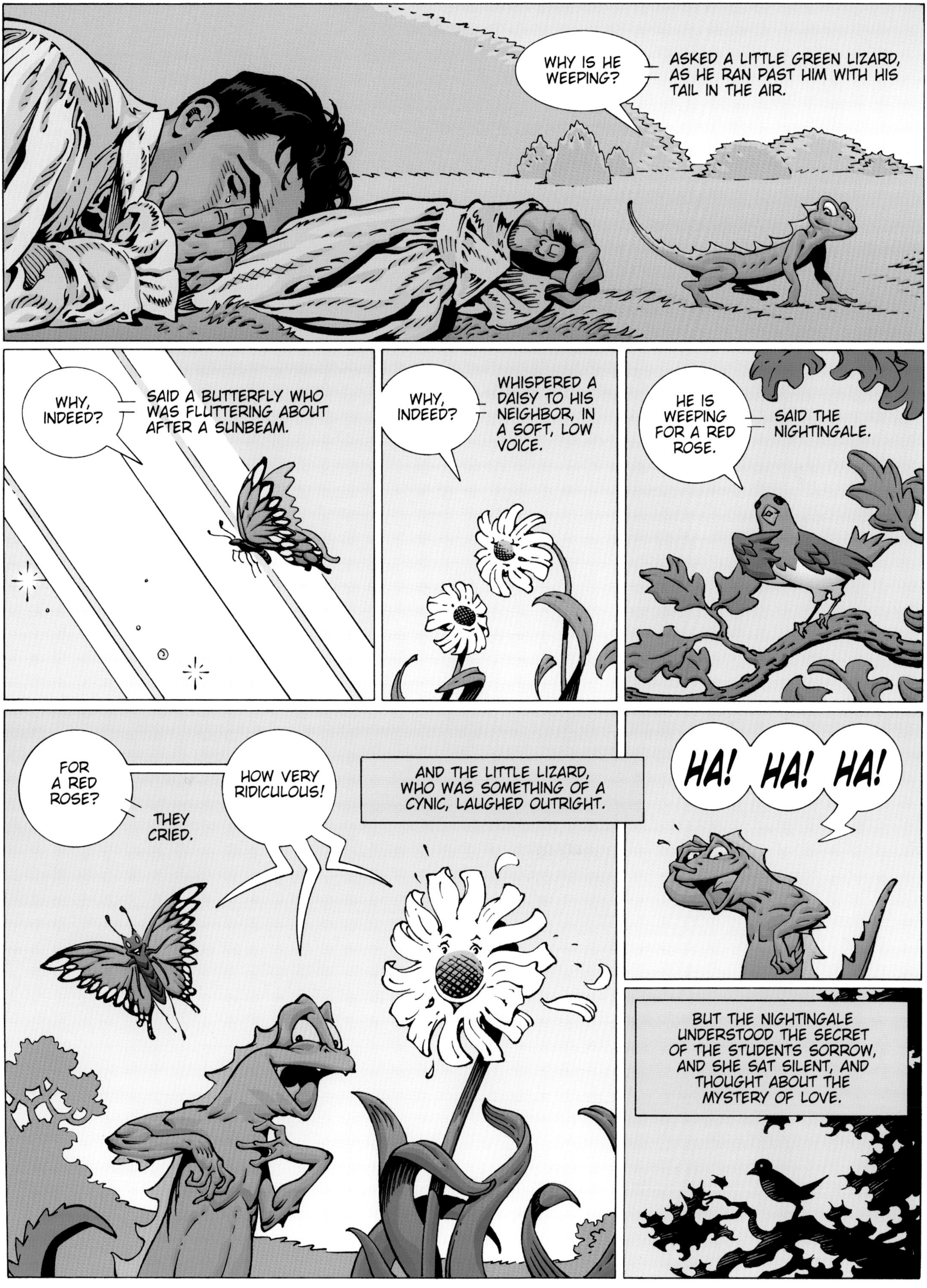
WHY IS HE WEEPING?
ASKED A LITTLE GREEN LIZARD, AS HE RAN PAST HIM WITH HIS TAIL IN THE AIR.
WHY, INDEED?
SAID A BUTTERFLY WHO WAS FLUTTERING ABOUT AFTER A SUNBEAM.
WHY, INDEED?
WHISPERED A DAISY TO HIS NEIGHBOR, IN A SOFT, LOW VOICE.
HE IS WEEPING FOR A RED ROSE.
SAID THE NIGHTINGALE.
FOR A RED ROSE?
THEY CRIED.
HOW VERY RIDICULOUS!
AND THE LITTLE LIZARD, WHO WAS SOMETHING OF A CYNIC, LAUGHED OUTRIGHT.
HA! HA! HA!
BUT THE NIGHTINGALE UNDERSTOOD THE SECRET OF THE STUDENTS SORROW, AND SHE SAT SILENT, AND THOUGHT ABOUT THE MYSTERY OF LOVE.

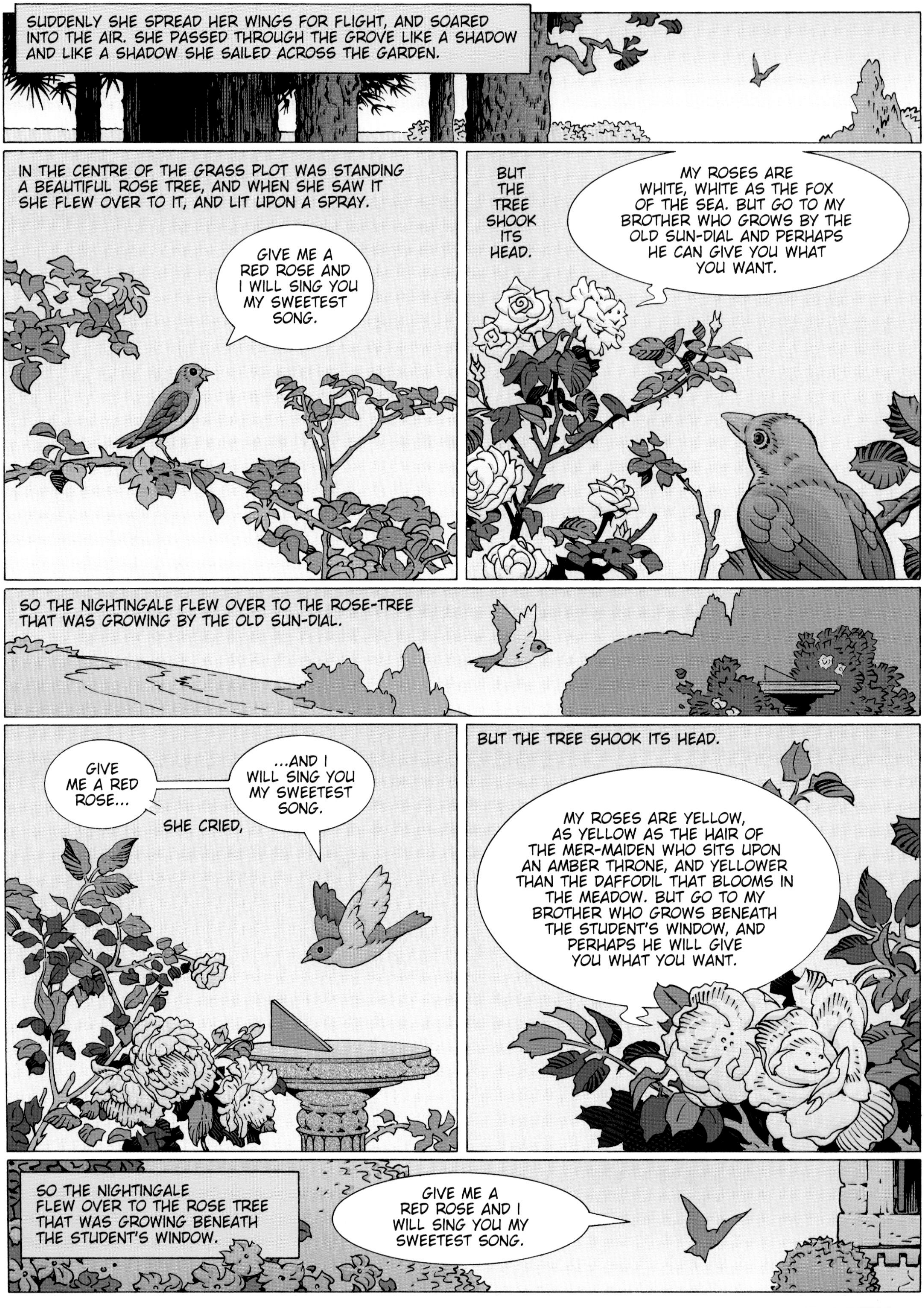
SUDDENLY SHE SPREAD HER WINGS FOR FLIGHT, AND SOARED INTO THE AIR. SHE PASSED THROUGH THE GROVE LIKE A SHADOW AND LIKE A SHADOW SHE SAILED ACROSS THE GARDEN.
IN THE CENTRE OF THE GRASS PLOT WAS STANDING A BEAUTIFUL ROSE TREE, AND WHEN SHE SAW IT SHE FLEW OVER TO IT, AND LIT UPON A SPRAY.
GIVE ME A RED ROSE AND I WILL SING YOU MY SWEETEST SONG.
BUT THE TREE SHOOK ITS HEAD.
MY ROSES ARE WHITE, WHITE AS THE FOX OF THE SEA. BUT GO TO MY BROTHER WHO GROWS BY THE OLD SUN-DIAL AND PERHAPS HE CAN GIVE YOU WHAT YOU WANT.
SO THE NIGHTINGALE FLEW OVER TO THE ROSE-TREE THAT WAS GROWING BY THE OLD SUN-DIAL.
GIVE ME A RED ROSE...
SHE CRIED,
...AND I WILL SING YOU MY SWEETEST SONG.
BUT THE TREE SHOOK ITS HEAD.
MY ROSES ARE YELLOW, AS YELLOW AS THE HAIR OF THE MER-MAIDEN WHO SITS UPON AN AMBER THRONE, AND YELLOWER THAN THE DAFFODIL THAT BLOOMS IN THE MEADOW. BUT GO TO MY BROTHER WHO GROWS BENEATH THE STUDENT'S WINDOW, AND PERHAPS HE WILL GIVE YOU WHAT YOU WANT.
SO THE NIGHTINGALE FLEW OVER TO THE ROSE TREE THAT WAS GROWING BENEATH THE STUDENT'S WINDOW.
GIVE ME A RED ROSE AND I WILL SING YOU MY SWEETEST SONG.

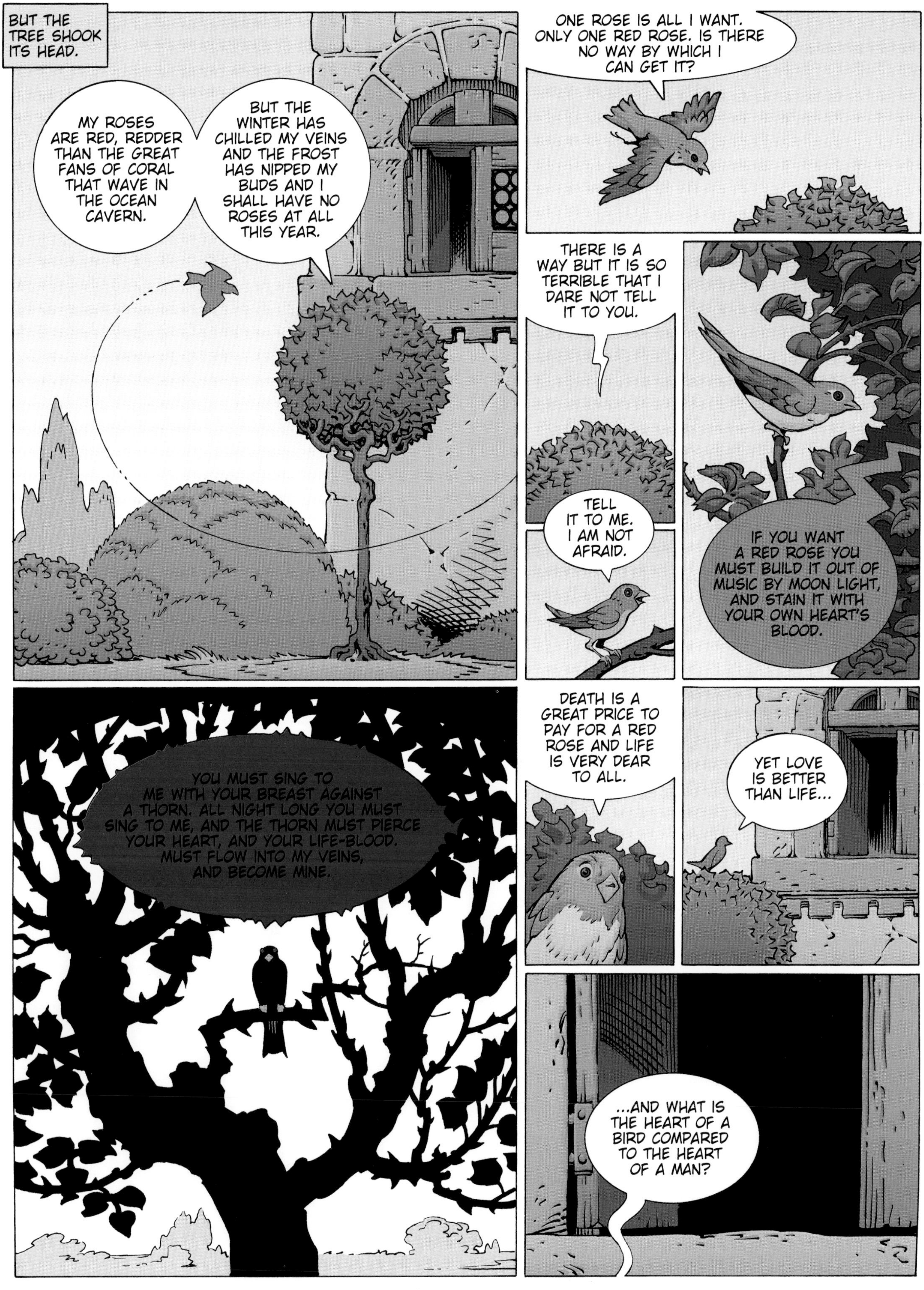
BUT THE TREE SHOOK ITS HEAD.
MY ROSES ARE RED, REDDER THAN THE GREAT FANS OF CORAL THAT WAVE IN THE OCEAN CAVERN.
BUT THE WINTER HAS CHILLED MY VEINS AND THE FROST HAS NIPPED MY BUDS AND I SHALL HAVE NO ROSES AT ALL THIS YEAR.
ONE ROSE IS ALL I WANT. ONLY ONE RED ROSE. IS THERE NO WAY BY WHICH I CAN GET IT?
THERE IS A WAY BUT IT IS SO TERRIBLE THAT I DARE NOT TELL IT TO YOU.
TELL IT TO ME. I AM NOT AFRAID.
IF YOU WANT A RED ROSE YOU MUST BUILD IT OUT OF MUSIC BY MOON LIGHT, AND STAIN IT WITH YOUR OWN HEART'S BLOOD.
YOU MUST SING TO ME WITH YOUR BREAST AGAINST A THORN. ALL NIGHT LONG YOU MUST SING TO ME, AND THE THORN MUST PIERCE YOUR HEART, AND YOUR LIFE-BLOOD. MUST FLOW INTO MY VEINS, AND BECOME MINE.
DEATH IS A GREAT PRICE TO PAY FOR A RED ROSE AND LIFE IS VERY DEAR TO ALL.
YET LOVE IS BETTER THAN LIFE...
...AND WHAT IS THE HEART OF A BIRD COMPARED TO THE HEART OF A MAN?

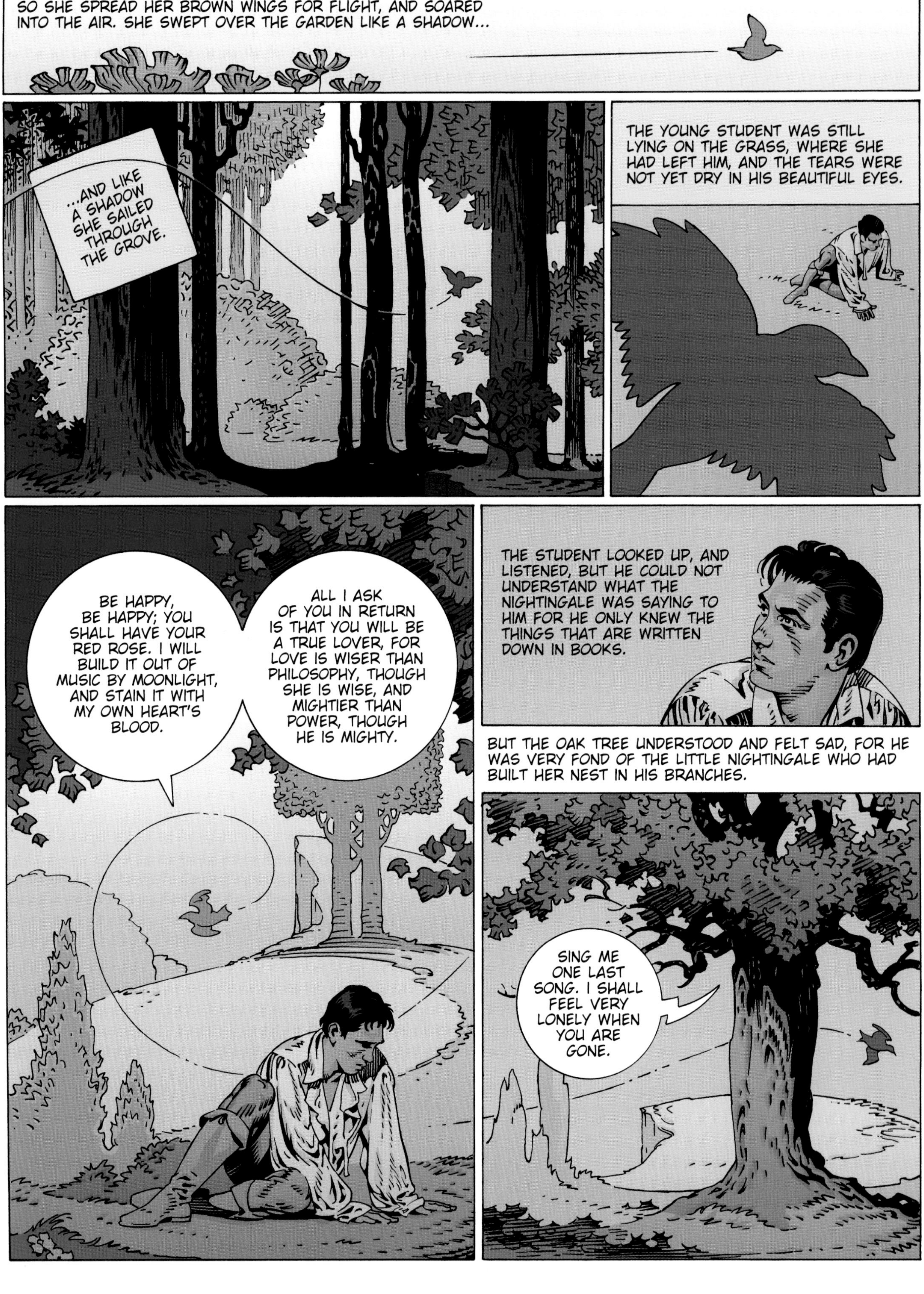
SO SHE SPREAD HER BROWN WINGS FOR FLIGHT, AND SOARED INTO THE AIR. SHE SWEPT OVER THE GARDEN LIKE A SHADOW...
...AND LIKE A SHADOW SHE SAILED THROUGH THE GROVE.
THE YOUNG STUDENT WAS STILL LYING ON THE GRASS, WHERE SHE HAD LEFT HIM, AND THE TEARS WERE NOT YET DRY IN HIS BEAUTIFUL EYES.
BE HAPPY, BE HAPPY; YOU SHALL HAVE YOUR RED ROSE. I WILL BUILD IT OUT OF MUSIC BY MOONLIGHT, AND STAIN IT WITH MY OWN HEART'S BLOOD.
ALL I ASK OF YOU IN RETURN IS THAT YOU WILL BE A TRUE LOVER, FOR LOVE IS WISER THAN PHILOSOPHY, THOUGH SHE IS WISE, AND MIGHTIER THAN POWER, THOUGH HE IS MIGHTY.
THE STUDENT LOOKED UP, AND LISTENED, BUT HE COULD NOT UNDERSTAND WHAT THE NIGHTINGALE WAS SAYING TO HIM FOR HE ONLY KNEW THE THINGS THAT ARE WRITTEN DOWN IN BOOKS.
BUT THE OAK TREE UNDERSTOOD AND FELT SAD, FOR HE WAS VERY FOND OF THE LITTLE NIGHTINGALE WHO HAD BUILT HER NEST IN HIS BRANCHES.
SING ME ONE LAST SONG. I SHALL FEEL VERY LONELY WHEN YOU ARE GONE.

SO THE NIGHTINBALE SANG TO THE OAK-TREE, AND HER VOICE WAS LIKE WATER BUBBLING FROM A SILVER JAR.

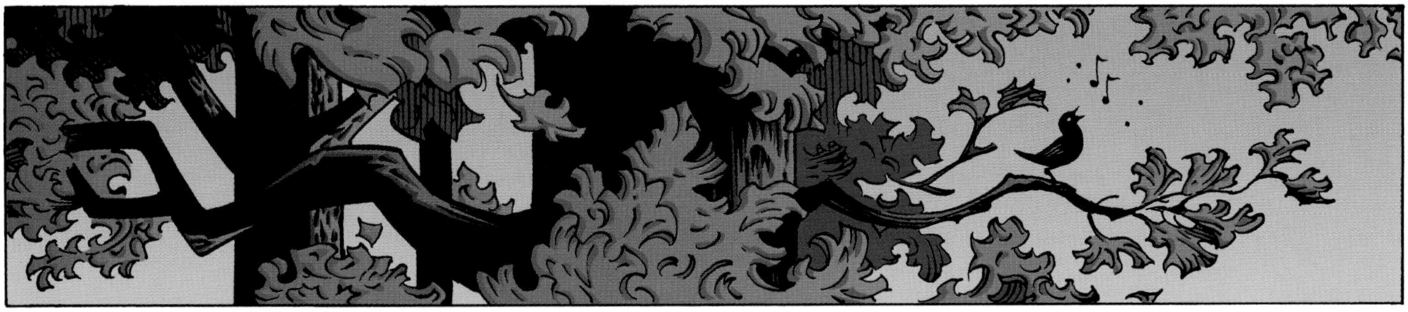

WHEN SHE HAD FINISHED HER SONG THE STUDENT GOT UP, AND PULLED A NOTE-BOOK OUT OF HIS POCKET.

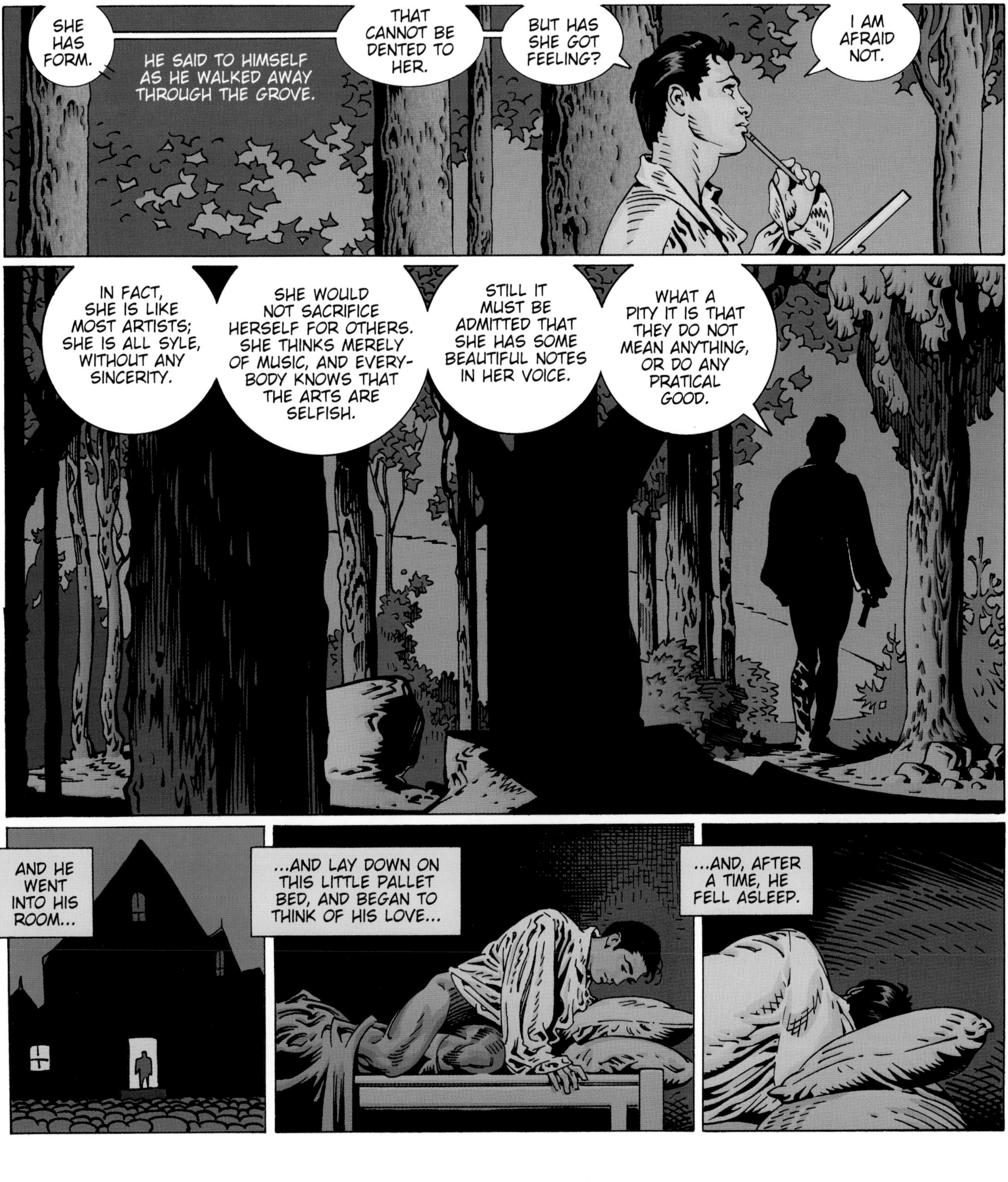

SHE HAS FORM.
HE SAID TO HIMSELF AS HE WALKED AWAY THROUGH THE GROVE.
THAT CANNOT BE DENTED TO HER.
BUT HAS SHE GOT FEELING?
I AM AFRAID NOT.
IN FACT, SHE IS LIKE MOST ARTISTS; SHE IS ALL SYLE, WITHOUT ANY SINCERITY.
SHE WOULD NOT SACRIFICE HERSELF FOR OTHERS. SHE THINKS MERELY OF MUSIC, AND EVERY-BODY KNOWS THAT THE ARTS ARE SELFISH.
STILL IT MUST BE ADMITTED THAT SHE HAS SOME BEAUTIFUL NOTES IN HER VOICE.
WHAT A PITY IT IS THAT THEY DO NOT MEAN ANYTHING, OR DO ANY PRATICAL GOOD.
AND HE WENT INTO HIS ROOM...
...AND LAY DOWN ON THIS LITTLE PALLET BED, AND BEGAN TO THINK OF HIS LOVE...
...AND, AFTER A TIME, HE FELL ASLEEP.

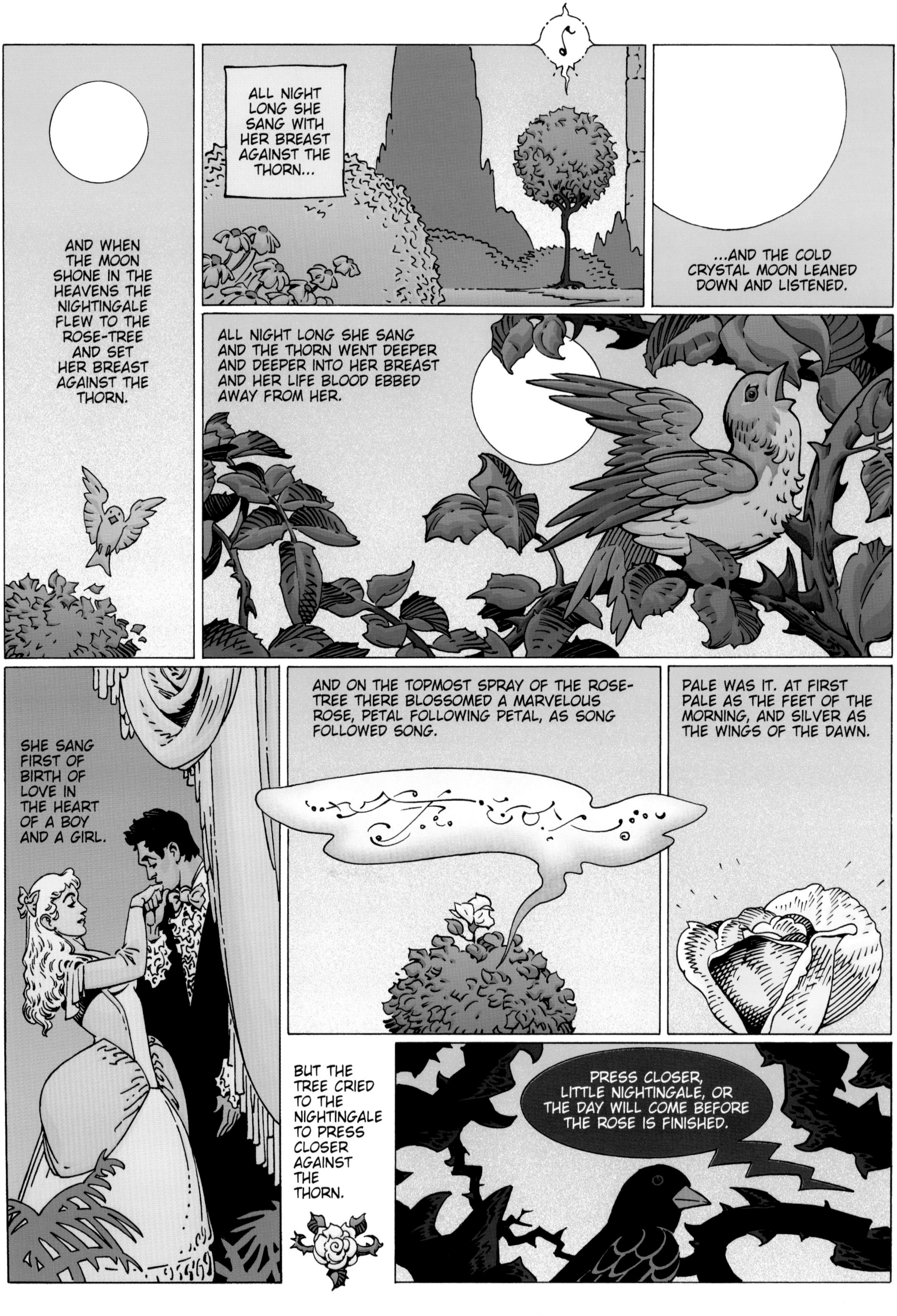
AND WHEN THE MOON SHONE IN THE HEAVENS THE NIGHTINGALE FLEW TO THE ROSE-TREE AND SET HER BREAST AGAINST THE THORN.
ALL NIGHT LONG SHE SANG WITH HER BREAST AGAINST THE THORN...
...AND THE COLD CRYSTAL MOON LEANED DOWN AND LISTENED.
ALL NIGHT LONG SHE SANG AND THE THORN WENT DEEPER AND DEEPER INTO HER BREAST AND HER LIFE BLOOD EBBED AWAY FROM HER.
SHE SANG FIRST OF BIRTH OF LOVE IN THE HEART OF A BOY AND A GIRL.
AND ON THE TOPMOST SPRAY OF THE ROSE-TREE THERE BLOSSOMED A MARVELOUS ROSE, PETAL FOLLOWING PETAL, AS SONG FOLLOWED SONG.
PALE WAS IT. AT FIRST PALE AS THE FEET OF THE MORNING, AND SILVER AS THE WINGS OF THE DAWN.
BUT THE TREE CRIED TO THE NIGHTINGALE TO PRESS CLOSER AGAINST THE THORN.
PRESS CLOSER, LITTLE NIGHTINGALE, OR THE DAY WILL COME BEFORE THE ROSE IS FINISHED.

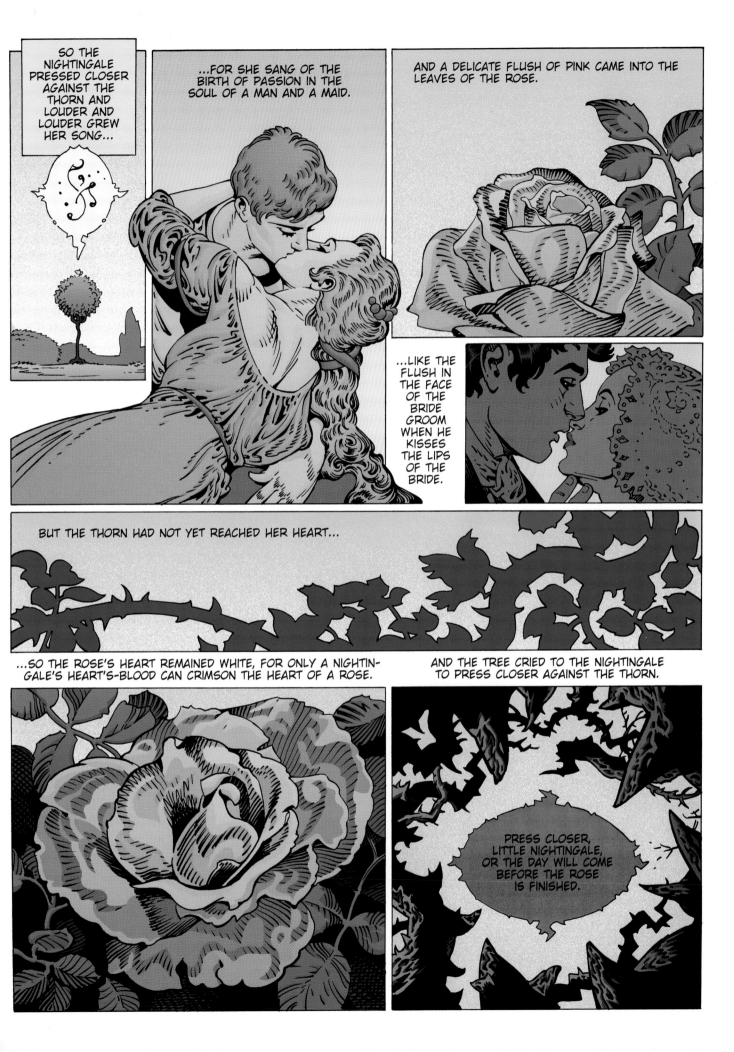

SO THE NIGHTINGALE PRESSED CLOSER AGAINST THE THORN AND LOUDER AND LOUDER GREW HER SONG...

...FOR SHE SANG OF THE BIRTH OF PASSION IN THE SOUL OF A MAN AND A MAID.

AND A DELICATE FLUSH OF PINK CAME INTO THE LEAVES OF THE ROSE.

...LIKE THE FLUSH IN THE FACE OF THE BRIDE GROOM WHEN HE KISSES THE LIPS OF THE BRIDE.

BUT THE THORN HAD NOT YET REACHED HER HEART...

...SO THE ROSE'S HEART REMAINED WHITE, FOR ONLY A NIGHTIN-GALE'S HEART'S-BLOOD CAN CRIMSON THE HEART OF A ROSE.

AND THE TREE CRIED TO THE NIGHTINGALE TO PRESS CLOSER AGAINST THE THORN.

PRESS CLOSER, LITTLE NIGHTINGALE, OR THE DAY WILL COME BEFORE THE ROSE IS FINISHED.

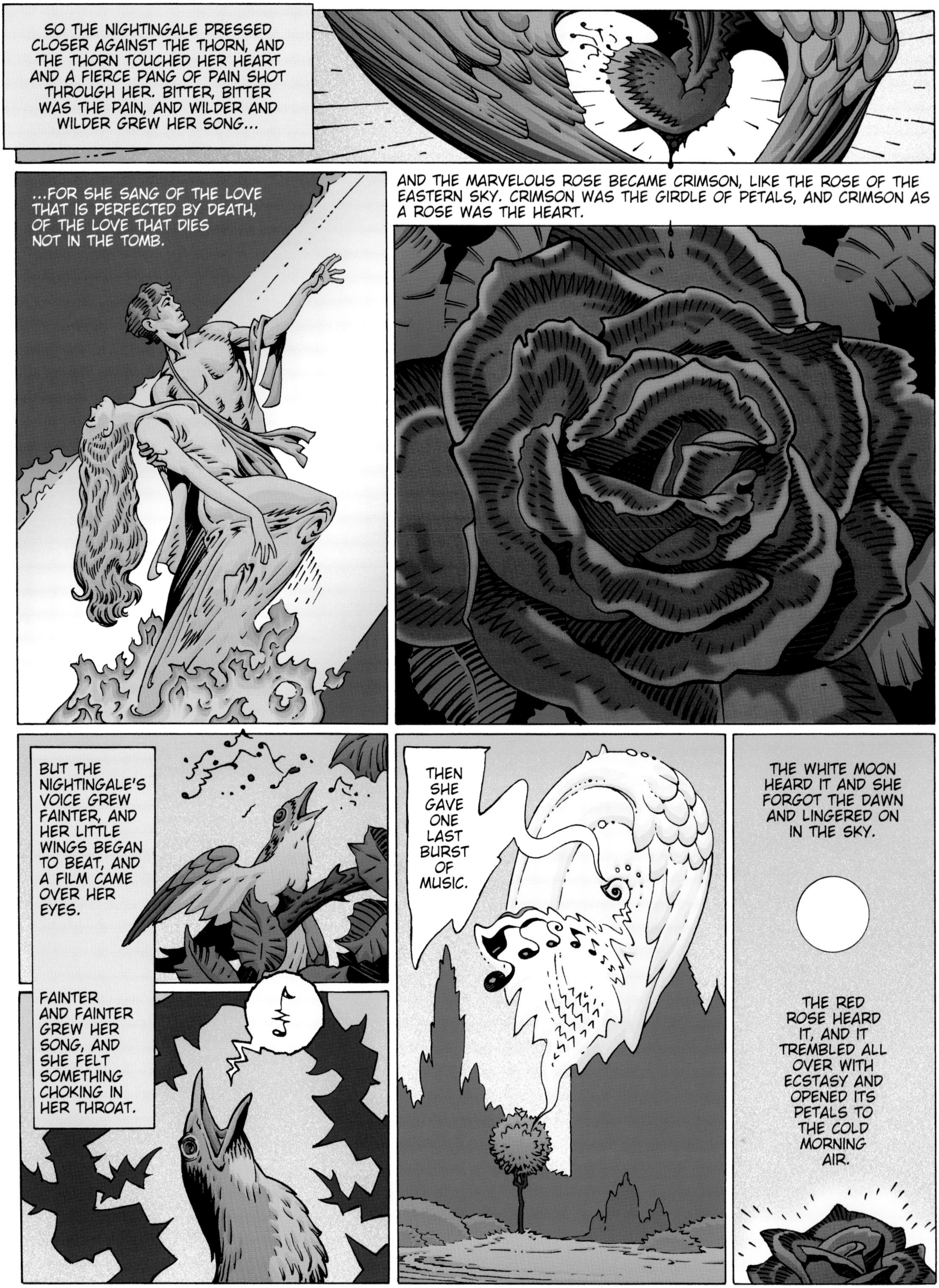
SO THE NIGHTINGALE PRESSED CLOSER AGAINST THE THORN, AND THE THORN TOUCHED HER HEART AND A FIERCE PANG OF PAIN SHOT THROUGH HER. BITTER, BITTER WAS THE PAIN, AND WILDER AND WILDER GREW HER SONG...
...FOR SHE SANG OF THE LOVE THAT IS PERFECTED BY DEATH, OF THE LOVE THAT DIES NOT IN THE TOMB.
AND THE MARVELOUS ROSE BECAME CRIMSON, LIKE THE ROSE OF THE EASTERN SKY. CRIMSON WAS THE GIRDLE OF PETALS, AND CRIMSON AS A ROSE WAS THE HEART.
BUT THE NIGHTINGALE'S VOICE GREW FAINTER, AND HER LITTLE WINGS BEGAN TO BEAT, AND A FILM CAME OVER HER EYES.
FAINTER AND FAINTER GREW HER SONG, AND SHE FELT SOMETHING CHOKING IN HER THROAT.
THEN SHE GAVE ONE LAST BURST OF MUSIC.
THE WHITE MOON HEARD IT AND SHE FORGOT THE DAWN AND LINGERED ON IN THE SKY.
THE RED ROSE HEARD IT, AND IT TREMBLED ALL OVER WITH ECSTASY AND OPENED ITS PETALS TO THE COLD MORNING AIR.

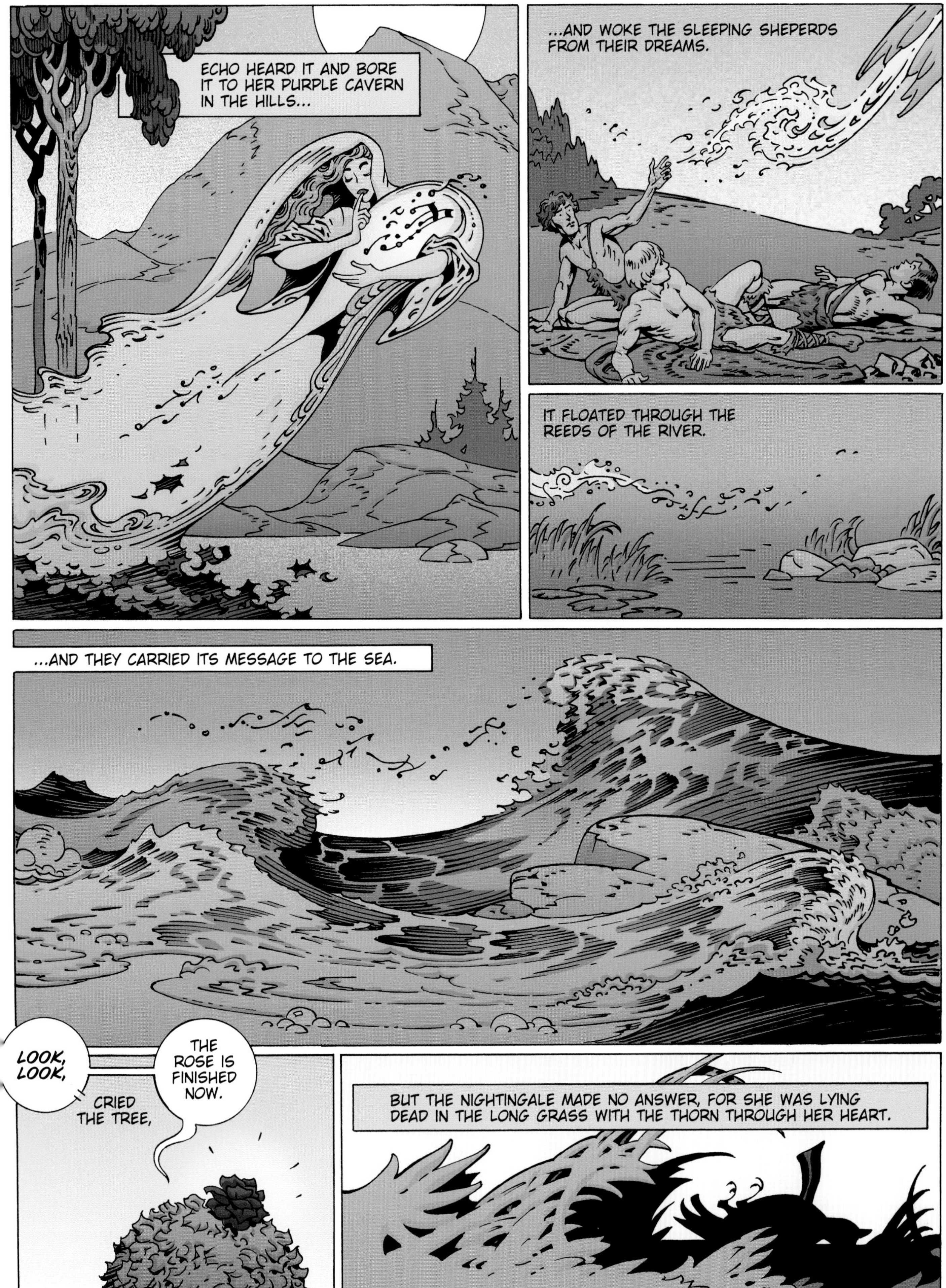
ECHO HEARD IT AND BORE IT TO HER PURPLE CAVERN IN THE HILLS...
...AND WOKE THE SLEEPING SHEPERDS FROM THEIR DREAMS.
IT FLOATED THROUGH THE REEDS OF THE RIVER.
...AND THEY CARRIED ITS MESSAGE TO THE SEA.
LOOK, LOOK,
CRIED THE TREE,
THE ROSE IS FINISHED NOW.
BUT THE NIGHTINGALE MADE NO ANSWER, FOR SHE WAS LYING DEAD IN THE LONG GRASS WITH THE THORN THROUGH HER HEART.

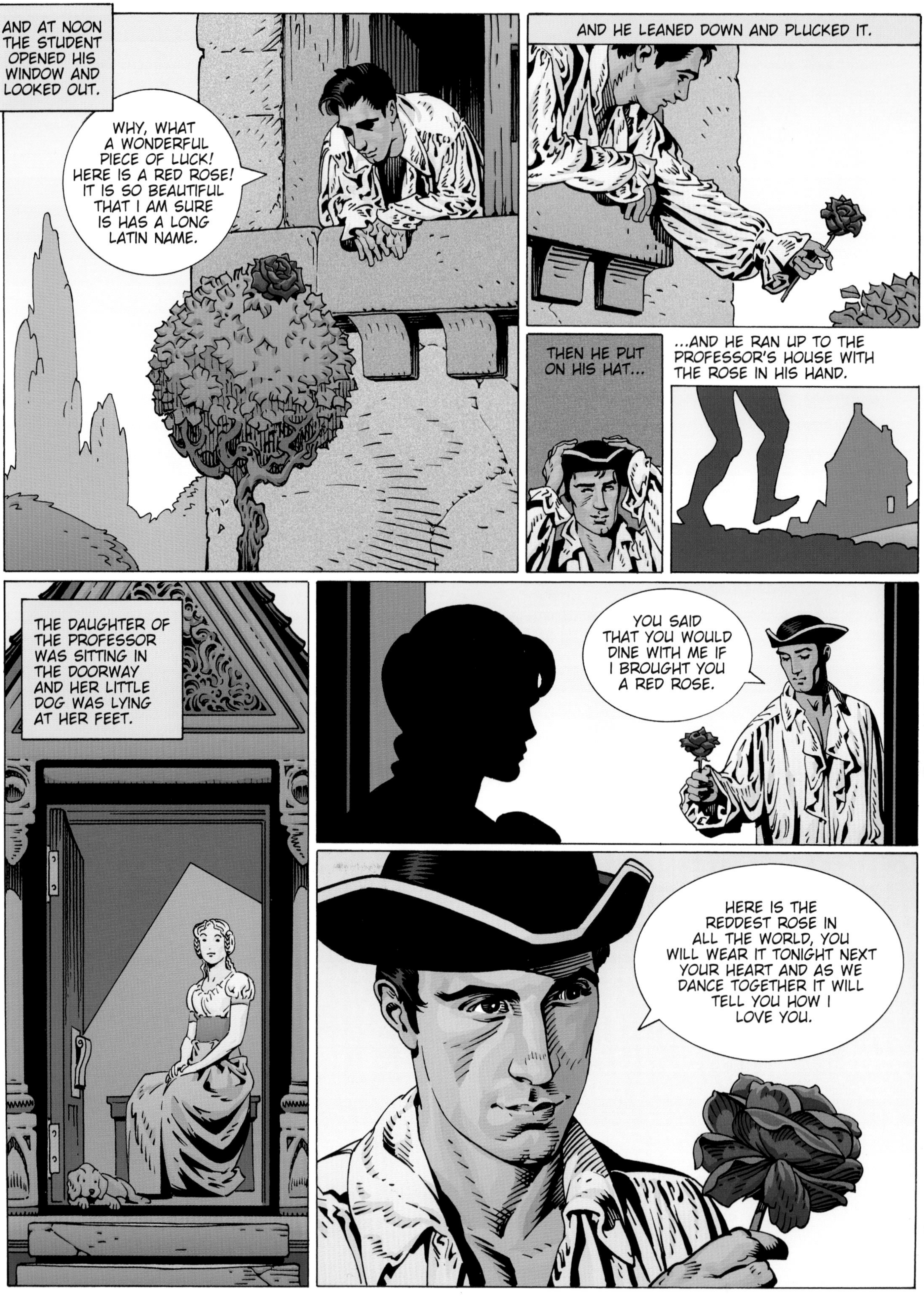
AND AT NOON THE STUDENT OPENED HIS WINDOW AND LOOKED OUT.
WHY, WHAT A WONDERFUL PIECE OF LUCK! HERE IS A RED ROSE! IT IS SO BEAUTIFUL THAT I AM SURE IS HAS A LONG LATIN NAME.
AND HE LEANED DOWN AND PLUCKED IT.
THEN HE PUT ON HIS HAT...
...AND HE RAN UP TO THE PROFESSOR'S HOUSE WITH THE ROSE IN HIS HAND.
THE DAUGHTER OF THE PROFESSOR WAS SITTING IN THE DOORWAY AND HER LITTLE DOG WAS LYING AT HER FEET.
YOU SAID THAT YOU WOULD DINE WITH ME IF I BROUGHT YOU A RED ROSE.
HERE IS THE REDDEST ROSE IN ALL THE WORLD, YOU WILL WEAR IT TONIGHT NEXT YOUR HEART AND AS WE DANCE TOGETHER IT WILL TELL YOU HOW I LOVE YOU.

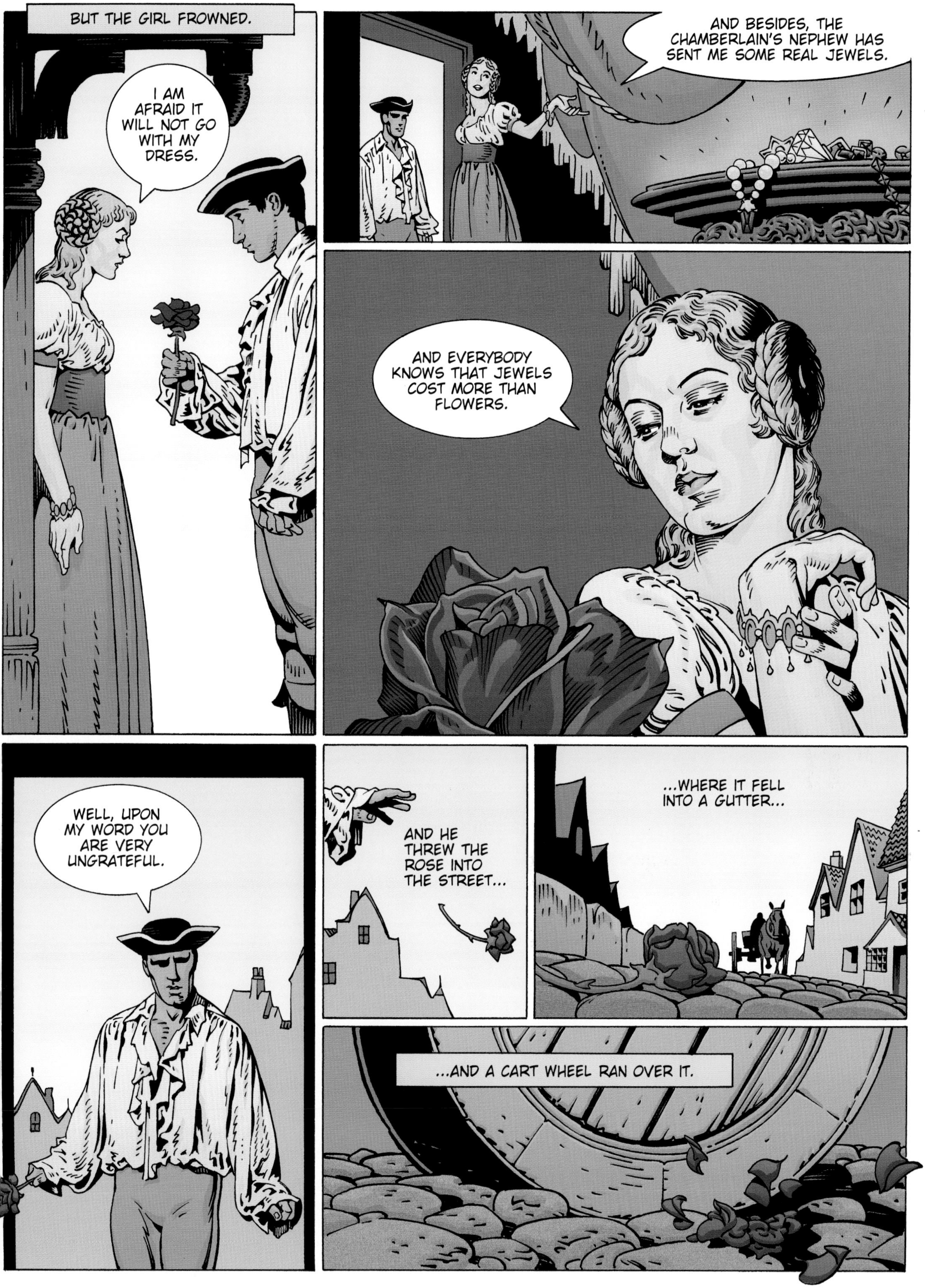
BUT THE GIRL FROWNED.
I AM AFRAID IT WILL NOT GO WITH MY DRESS.
AND BESIDES, THE CHAMBERLAIN'S NEPHEW HAS SENT ME SOME REAL JEWELS.
AND EVERYBODY KNOWS THAT JEWELS COST MORE THAN FLOWERS.
WELL, UPON MY WORD YOU ARE VERY UNGRATEFUL.
AND HE THREW THE ROSE INTO THE STREET...
...WHERE IT FELL INTO A GUTTER...
...AND A CART WHEEL RAN OVER IT.

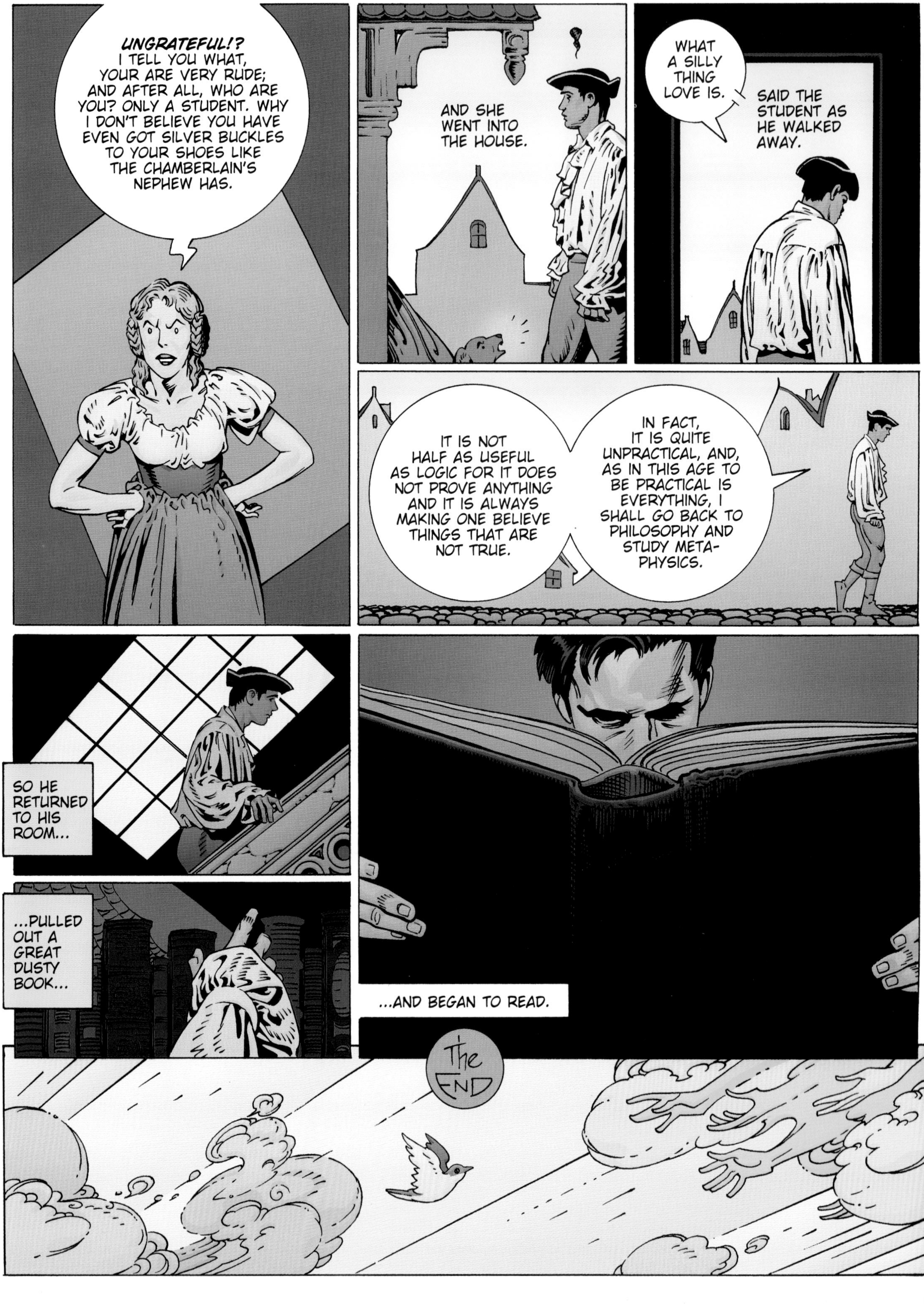
UNGRATEFUL!? I TELL YOU WHAT, YOUR ARE VERY RUDE; AND AFTER ALL, WHO ARE YOU? ONLY A STUDENT. WHY I DON'T BELIEVE YOU HAVE EVEN GOT SILVER BUCKLES TO YOUR SHOES LIKE THE CHAMBERLAIN'S NEPHEW HAS.
AND SHE WENT INTO THE HOUSE.
WHAT A SILLY THING LOVE IS.
SAID THE STUDENT AS HE WALKED AWAY.
IT IS NOT HALF AS USEFUL AS LOGIC FOR IT DOES NOT PROVE ANYTHING AND IT IS ALWAYS MAKING ONE BELIEVE THINGS THAT ARE NOT TRUE.
IN FACT, IT IS QUITE UNPRACTICAL, AND, AS IN THIS AGE TO BE PRACTICAL IS EVERYTHING, I SHALL GO BACK TO PHILOSOPHY AND STUDY META-PHYSICS.
SO HE RETURNED TO HIS ROOM...
...PULLED OUT A GREAT DUSTY BOOK...
...AND BEGAN TO READ.
The END